Trouble,

Lucas had thought when the mother and child arrived at his ranch.

Now he groaned at the innocence of the word. *Trouble* didn't even begin to describe what he was in for.

He could still hear her soft voice echoing through his mind, floating down from the spare room upstairs where she and the little boy were settling in for the night. And his body still hummed from her sweet scent.

It had been a while—a long while—since he'd reacted so swiftly to any woman. But Lucas had ignored that warning—so he hadn't even noticed the approaching storm about to snow them in together.

Hell, she wasn't even pretty. Not in the usual ways—the things men looked for in a woman. Her floppy sweatshirt wasn't hiding anything remotely voluptuous.

Lucas grunted his displeasure. She and the boy didn't belong here.

A woman was nothin' but…trouble.

Dear Reader,

You asked for more ROYALLY WED titles and you've
got them! For the next four months we've brought back
the Stanbury family—first introduced in a short story by
Carla Cassidy on our eHarlequin.com Web site. Be sure to
check the archives to find Nicholas's story! But don't forget to
pick up Stella Bagwell's *The Expectant Princess* and discover
the involving story of the disappearance of King Michael.

Other treats this month include Marie Ferrarella's one
hundredth title for Silhouette Books! This wonderful, charming
and emotional writer shows her trademark warmth and humor
in *Rough Around the Edges*. Luckily for all her devoted readers,
Marie has at least another hundred plots bubbling in her
imagination, and we'll be seeing more from her in many of
our Silhouette lines.

Then we've got Karen Rose Smith's *Tall, Dark & True*
about a strong, silent sheriff who can't bear to keep quiet
about his feelings any longer. And Donna Clayton's heroine
asks *Who Will Father My Baby?*—and gets a surprising answer.
No Place Like Home by Robin Nicholas is a delightful read
that reminds us of an all-time favorite movie—I'll let you guess
which one! And don't forget first-time author Roxann Delaney's
debut title, *Rachel's Rescuer*.

Next month be sure to return for *The Blacksheep Prince's
Bride* by Martha Shields, the next of the ROYALLY WED
series. Also returning are popular authors Judy Christenberry
and Elizabeth August.

Happy reading!

Mary-Theresa Hussey

Mary-Theresa Hussey
Senior Editor

Please address questions and book requests to:
Silhouette Reader Service
U.S.: 3010 Walden Ave., P.O. Box 1325, Buffalo, NY 14269
Canadian: P.O. Box 609, Fort Erie, Ont. L2A 5X3

Rachel's Rescuer

ROXANN DELANEY

SILHOUETTE *Romance*®

Published by Silhouette Books

America's Publisher of Contemporary Romance

With bunches of love to the Ditzy Chix, who kept at me
until it happened. Thank you. And to my four lovely
daughters, who make my life the best.

 SILHOUETTE BOOKS

ISBN 0-373-19509-5

RACHEL'S RESCUER

ROXANN DELANEY

lives on a farm in south-central Kansas and is the mother of four daughters. The 1999 Maggie Award winner spent many hours spinning tales while driving a wheat truck to the grain elevator during harvest. Though she and her family are no longer actively farming, their current menagerie of dogs, cats and one lop-eared rabbit named Rudy manages to keep them busy. A theater buff, Roxann once established a community theater in her hometown, and both acted in and directed the productions, as well as serving on the board of directors. But writing is her first love, and she's thrilled to have followed her yellow brick road to the land of Silhouette Romance.

Dear Reader,

Like many of you, I'm a mom. And like most moms, I know my four daughters well. When I told them I'd sold my first book, their reactions were varied, as I'd expected. But whether it was a simple "That's nice, Mom," from the oldest or "I'm going to be a writer, just like you!" from the youngest, they all enjoyed sharing in the champagne-toast celebration. Somehow, I knew they would. That's the way moms are. *They* think that's magic. We know better.

Magic. That's the word that comes to mind when I think of what writers refer to as "The Call." Those magical words "We'd like to buy your book" can be likened only to hearing the doctor say, "Congratulations! You're pregnant!" With one sentence, the world becomes a strange but beautiful place. Then, like pregnancy, we wait to actually see our "baby" born, when we hold the book in our hands. The joy is indescribable, even for a writer.

So curl up in your favorite reading spot and hold my "baby." May it bring you laughter, may it bring a tear, but most of all, may it bring you joy.

Ruyann Delaney

Chapter One

Squinting into the crimson glare quickly disappearing behind the building clouds of an approaching winter storm, Lucas Callahan watched twin columns of dust race along the usually deserted ranch road.

"What the hell—"

Releasing the small calf he'd just tagged, he stood in silence and watched the first of two cars come to a dirt-spewing halt, missing the fence in front of the sprawling two-story house by inches. A woman climbed from the older model, red sports car, panic written all over her. She stood frozen to the spot when the tan cruiser of the county sheriff stopped, nearly crashing into her car.

Sheriff Ben Tatum climbed out of his vehicle and slammed his hat on his head. He strode forward, badge bouncing on his barrel chest. Coming to a stop directly in front of the woman, he planted his fists on his hips, legs spread wide. "Lady, what the hell do you think you're doin'?"

Lucas stepped back into the deepening shadow of the barn and waited. From his vantage point, he could clearly see the scene unfolding in the yard, even though the sun continued its slow descent, and the sky had begun to darken. He wanted to hear what the woman had to say, but he didn't want to be seen. Ben would handle the stranger better than he could. The two men had known each other all their lives, being born a few days apart, thirty-two years earlier.

"I...you..." She tugged at the hem of a too large sweatshirt, her nervous glance sweeping past Ben and lingering on her car. Squaring her shoulders, she faced him and lifted her chin. "I guess I'm lost."

Ben knuckled back the brim of his hat. "Don't you know you should pull over when an officer attempts to stop you?"

Her chin went up another notch, and she stiffened. "What did I do wrong?"

"Nothin'." Ben walked around to the back of her car and leaned down.

The woman took a faltering step to follow, but brought herself up short when he straightened, a license plate in his hand. Her mouth opened once, then snapped shut.

He rounded the fender and held out the tag. "This was just flappin' in the breeze, about to fall off. Drivin' around without plates will get you in trouble, even here in Montana."

"You came after me with your lights flashing because my license tag was loose?"

Ben's stern countenance deepened to a frown. "So you did see me behind you. Next time an officer attempts to stop you, you stop."

Her head lowered. "Yes, sir."

Impatient to get back to his chores before dark settled in and the storm put a halt to the work, Lucas stepped out of the shadows. "I've got some plate screws."

The woman jumped, and her hand flew to her throat. "How long have you been there?" she demanded.

Lucas took three strides in her direction and stopped at the corral fence. "Long enough."

Brilliant blue eyes narrowed. "And what does that mean?"

Lucas sucked in a breath at the sight of those eyes. "I saw you flyin' up the road."

She tugged on her shirt again, her nervous gaze going to the car for the second time. "I was lost."

"You've got a bigger problem than that, little lady." Ben pointed to the front tire of her car, where a soft hiss could be heard.

"Flat," Lucas grumbled. He wanted her gone, blue eyes and all. Something was wrong, and he didn't want to know what it was. He wanted her off the Blue Sage. "We'll get it changed, and you can be on your way."

"I—I don't have a spare."

Before Lucas could reply with a string of words unfit for a woman's ears, Ben interrupted. "Where was it you said you were headed?"

Looking up, she tensed again. "I didn't say."

It couldn't have been clearer that something was going on. Lucas glimpsed fear beneath the stubborn stance. He wondered if Ben noticed it. The sheriff might look a little slow to some, but the man didn't let much get by him.

Lucas didn't take his eyes off her. He quickly reminded himself that strangers couldn't be trusted in the middle of nowhere. Even isolated areas like the Blue Sage Ranch were known to have their share of con artists and other misbegotten vermin. Never a trusting soul, especially when it came to women, he wouldn't put it past her to be part of some sort of scam.

And he didn't welcome the interruption. The weather was expected to get bad—real bad. The woman needed to be on her way. *The sooner the better.*

Lucas let his gaze take a slow journey over the stranger, checking out the chestnut brown of her hair and the slender neck holding up an obstinate chin. Skipping over the loose-fitting shirt, his gaze lingered on her slim hips and long legs encased in threadbare blue jeans. A pair of dirty, time-worn tennis shoes finished the trip.

"If you're lost, I'll give you directions," Ben was saying, jerking Lucas's attention away from the leisurely tour of her body.

"Just tell me where and how far I am from Deerfork," the woman replied. "I'll find my way from there."

"You're headed to Deerfork?"

She hesitated. "Sort of."

"Near Deerfork?"

Nodding, she said nothing.

"I'll give Willie a call and have him bring the tow truck out," Ben said, then turned for his patrol car.

"If you tell me where you're headed, I can give you better directions," Lucas offered, his patience wearing thin. His suspicion mounted as he watched her twist her fingers in the hem of her shirt. She was scared. And not just of the law.

"I'm headed to see my—my friend," she finally answered. "She and her husband live near Deerfork. I must have taken a wrong turn."

The glare she directed at him nearly brought a smile to his lips. She was too easily riled. *And too pretty when she was.* He shook off the thought. "A name would give me somethin' to go on."

Lowering her head, she hid her expression behind a curtain of hair. "Richmond. Jenny Richmond."

He swore under his breath. "Jen and Pete left a couple of weeks ago for a vacation."

"Oh, no!" She swayed, wrapping her arms around her middle.

He gripped the fence in front of him to keep from rushing to her. No way was he getting involved. "You okay?"

Her chin lifted again. "I'll be on my way, as soon as the tow truck gets here."

While they glared at each other, Ben returned. "There's been an accident over on I-15 I've gotta get to. Willie's on his way there now." He turned to the woman. "You'll have to stay here, until he's done and can get here."

"Hold on!" Vaulting the fence and crossing the short distance to where the pair stood, Lucas addressed them both. "She can ride back with you, and Willie can get her car tomorrow. We'll find her a place to stay in Deerfork."

The wind kicked up, swirling dirt into the sharply cooling air around them. Gesturing with a nod of his head, Ben led Lucas to the cruiser. "She'll have to stay here, Lucas, unless you can take her into Deerfork."

"Can't. I've got a new bull calf I have to keep an eye on. You'll have to take her."

"Nope, can't do it. I've gotta get to that accident." Ben climbed into his car and rolled down the window, shaking his head. "Bunch o' wild kids drivin' too fast. When a storm's a'comin', all hell breaks loose. Nothin' but trouble."

"I'd say *she's* trouble." Lucas silently counted to five as Ben started the engine. "She's not stayin' here, and that's—"

"Mom?"

He spun around at the sound of the voice, while Ben pulled out of the drive. Too preoccupied with this new development to try to stop the sheriff, Lucas squinted into the blowing dust to see the driver's door of the woman's car swing open. Unable to make out who it was, he rounded the back of the car and stopped in his tracks.

"It's all right," the woman said, pulling a small boy of about five or six close to her. With her arms wrapped possessively around the youngster, she glared at Lucas.

Eyes full of distrust, the boy looked up at him. "Who's he?"

If his life depended on it, Lucas couldn't have uttered a single word. After a moment of dead silence, he cleared his throat and forced himself to speak. "I'm Lucas Callahan. And your name is?"

"Cody."

Promising himself the satisfaction of blasting Ben the next time he saw him, Lucas looked at the sky, then nodded. "Guess we'd better get to the house."

"Isn't there something else we can do? We can't stay here." The woman kept the boy close and shivered, but whether from fear or cold, Lucas couldn't be sure.

"You'll have to," he stated, pointing them toward the porch and silently damning his luck. The sky had darkened to near black, and fat snowflakes whirled in the wind with the dust. "In thirty minutes, nobody'll be able to get to the county road."

And he was stuck with a woman and a kid for God knew how long.

Rachel Harris didn't know if her legs would carry her to the house. She could feel the man's eyes on her, and she knew he didn't trust her. She couldn't blame him. In the same situation, she would react the same way. She had to be careful. Suspicious people asked questions. Questions she couldn't answer. Not if she wanted to keep Cody safe.

Blinking at the lights shining brightly inside the house, she entered the kitchen.

"Coffee?" the cowboy asked and pulled out two chairs from a large table.

Uncertainty gnawed at her, but she nodded and took the seat he offered. Daring a glance at the scowling man who crossed the roomy kitchen with long, bold strides, Rachel's breath caught. Outside, the light had grown too dim to notice much by the time she'd realized he was there, and she had been too scared after that to pay much attention. But now that she could see him, if only from the back, she wished she had jumped in the car and taken off, flat tire and all.

A good six feet plus tall, Lucas Callahan resembled the devil himself. Beneath his black hat, thick dark hair curled against a deeply tanned neck and touched the collar of his matching black shirt. From the back,

he looked formidable. From the front, she guessed
he'd be frightening. The expanse of his shoulders was
broad enough to lean on and feel safe, but didn't look
in the least bit inviting. Narrow-hipped and long-
legged, he reminded her of a piece of onyx. Hard.
Cold.

"Thank you," she whispered, when he set a cup of
coffee before her. After breathing in the comforting
aroma, she offered a grateful smile. She hadn't had
any coffee since yesterday morning, and she craved it.
But she had less than forty dollars, and she hadn't
wanted to spend even a little on a selfish cup of coffee.
She'd counted on Jenny being home. Disappointment
brought the walls of desperation closing in on her. In
her twenty-seven years, she had felt many things. This
bordered on the worst.

Lucas set a glass of milk in front of Cody, then
turned back to a row of cabinets and rummaged
through them. With a soft grunt of what must have
been satisfaction, he tossed a half-empty package of
cookies onto the table.

"Better not eat all of them. They may have to last
a few days."

Cody looked at Rachel, who answered the question
in his eyes with a smile. He took one cookie, eating
it slowly and carefully, as if it were something strange
and exotic.

Rachel watched him, her love for her son overcom-
ing her fear. He'd been so good, never once complain-
ing about being stuck in the car for days on end. They
had even slept in it for the past two nights, so they
wouldn't risk running out of money. But instead of
making it to her childhood friend's the way she had
planned, here she was, sitting in the comfy but unfa-

miliar kitchen of a strange man. After seeing the friendly familiarity between him and the sheriff, her instincts told her she and her son were probably safe. Hadn't it been the sheriff who had suggested she stay? She wasn't scared, but she was certainly aware of the man across the room. And she couldn't explain it.

Wrapping her hands around the hot cup in front of her, she looked up. "Do you know when Jenny and Pete will be back?"

He didn't look at her. "Last I heard, they might be gone for a month."

"A month!" Her heart sank to her toes. That meant another two weeks. Her cash wouldn't last more than a day or two at the most, and she couldn't risk using her credit cards. They were too easy to trace when someone had the means to do it. And Steven's parents did. Somehow, she would have to find a place to stay until Jenny returned. But when would she be able to leave?

She dared another look at Lucas Callahan. He wore his hat pulled so low over his face, she couldn't be sure where his attention was focused, but the distinct burning in her cheeks narrowed her guess. He hadn't moved since he'd tossed the package of cookies, except to lean back against the counter, plant one big, booted foot over the other, and cross his arms on his chest. The stance only made him look more unapproachable. So why did she feel drawn to him?

Rachel turned her focus back to her coffee and gathered her strength. "We can drive to Great Falls, as soon as the tire is repaired. How long do you think the storm will last? Is there a chance we can leave tonight?"

"Doubt it," Lucas answered. "Depends on how

much snow we get and how hard the wind blows. If it keeps up, it'll be a few days before you can get out of here.''

Her heart sank deeper, and she couldn't help but notice the howl of that wind beyond the quiet of the snug room. A shiver went through her, and she told herself it was caused by the eerie sound, not by the fact that she could feel a pair of eyes boring into her. She hadn't seen those eyes in the light yet, but she felt certain they would be cold, like the owner. Why was he so unfriendly? So…hostile? Most people were wary of strangers, but didn't he realize she hadn't chosen to be stranded?

"Before it gets any worse, I'd better get your car moved so it doesn't get buried. Anything you need from it?"

She thought of the four suitcases and the boxes in the trunk containing everything they hadn't had to leave behind. If he saw those, he would know for sure this wasn't a pleasure trip for a short visit to a friend. He might not press for answers, at least not right away, but he would soon. Luckily, she had kept one small bag handy.

"There's a backpack behind the seat," she answered. "And Cody's coat. Some blankets, too. The keys are in the ignition."

He nodded and shoved away from the counter, his long strides taking him quickly past her to the door. "You won't need the blankets. There's plenty of extra bedrooms here. I'll get a room fixed up for the two of you."

"Thank you." She kept her gaze averted. Something about him, when he walked by her, had her nerve endings tingling.

"It may be a while. I've got stock to check." He put on his hat and shrugged into a heavy coat. For a moment, he hesitated. "Would you mind stirring that pot on the stove?"

"Of course not." She stood and, as he hurried out the door, she lifted the tight-fitting lid, letting the aroma of the contents into the room. Dipping a long wooden spoon into the kettle, she inhaled. The scent warmed her heart. "Mmmm. Chicken soup."

"Mom?"

She finished stirring and replaced the lid. "What is it, Cody?"

"When are we going to get to Jenny's?"

"In a few days." Rachel moved to where he sat at the table, his empty glass sitting amid a small scattering of cookie crumbs. She smoothed his dark hair and rubbed her hand along his neck, hoping to soothe the worry in his eyes. She didn't want Cody looking over his shoulder the way she'd been forced to for the past six months. If only she had called Jenny to warn her they were coming. But they'd had to leave so quickly this time.

"Are we going to stay here until then?" he asked, his hazel eyes too wise for a six-year-old.

"We'll find someplace else as soon as it clears up." *Somehow.* But if the cowboy's prediction of the weather proved correct, she didn't have a choice. She and Cody would have to stay.

Knowing worry wouldn't gain her anything, she set herself in motion, searching the cabinets for bowls and something to go with the soup.

A short time later, the door behind her swung open, banging into the wall and bringing in both a gust of snow-laden wind and Lucas. She jumped at the sound, but forced her attention to the display of food in front of her, ignoring the rough whisper of denim and the clomp of boots on the tile floor. She had to be dead tired, she told herself, to be unable to keep her curiosity at bay. And that's all it was. Simple curiosity. But even that frightened her. Still, it didn't stop her from glancing over her shoulder for another peek.

Whipping off his hat, he stomped his feet to rid his boots of their covering of snow and slapped his hat on his leg. "Doesn't look too good out there."

She hurried to fix a plate of crackers she had found, while he hung his coat and hat on a peg behind the door. Without another word, he approached the table and set her red nylon backpack and Cody's coat on an empty chair.

Shoving aside her disappointment of the forecast, she found three bowls, filled them, and placed everything on the table. "I don't know what else you planned to have."

"That's about it. Hope it'll be enough for you two."

"It's fine." She added a smile and sat down. "It smells delicious."

The only available chair was to her right, at the end of the table. It was only natural to look in that direction when he moved to it. But not so natural for her heart to stop for a brief moment when their gazes met. Without his hat, she was able to see him clearly for the first time. Dark, nearly black eyes gazed into hers, leaving her breathless.

After a moment that seemed like an eternity, she ducked her head, and then watched him crumble a huge handful of crackers into his bowl. Cody, she noticed, watched, too, and then did the same to his own soup. Her son needed a male figure in his life. It had been two years since Steven's death, and Cody didn't remember much about his dad. Since then, she had been too busy earning a living to give much thought to Cody's other needs, beyond keeping a roof over his head and food in his stomach. She spent every minute she could with him, though, being both mother and father. She would never let anyone take him from her, no matter how far or how long she had to run.

"I didn't catch your name."

At the sound of his voice, a ball of lead formed in her stomach. She couldn't give him her name, but she couldn't ignore the request either. Not when he'd opened his home to her and Cody.

"It's Rachel."

"Rachel what?" he asked, pinning her with those dark eyes.

"Rachel...Stevens," she replied, using her husband's first name for a last. Scolding herself for not thinking ahead, she stood and moved away from the table, her hands shaking. She hated lying, especially in front of Cody. Later she would explain to him why she'd done it. And explain it in a way that wouldn't frighten him. She needed to stay on her toes if she wanted to keep them both safe.

Trouble, he'd told Ben earlier. Lucas groaned at the innocence of the word. Trouble didn't even begin to describe what he was in for.

He could still hear her voice, floating down from the spare room upstairs where they were settling in for the night. Her name kept echoing through his mind like a soft whisper. And his body still hummed. It had been a while—a long while—since he'd reacted so swiftly to any woman. In fact, it was a long stretch to remember any time he had even come close.

He had ignored the first warning at the corral when he'd looked down into the eyes of an angel, blue as the wide Montana sky on a summer afternoon. After that moment, he hadn't noticed the chill of the evening or the cold of the approaching storm.

In the light of the kitchen, he'd gotten a good look and knew she didn't have the soft, full curves of the women who had once attracted his attention. In spite of the floppy sweatshirt, he could see she wasn't hiding anything remotely voluptuous. He'd always had a soft spot for well-endowed women. The woman now making herself comfortable in one of the spare rooms didn't possess that particular asset.

And still he hadn't been able to stop looking at her.

"Hell," he muttered, followed by a string of words that would make a sailor blush. He stepped into the ranch office and closed the door behind him. Walking to the window, he stared out into the stormy night, seeing nothing but the image of the woman temporarily sharing his home.

Hell, she isn't even pretty. Not in the usual way. Not in the way that counted, the things men looked for in a woman. Her mouth was too wide, her nose was too short and her eyes were too...blue. Way too blue.

When the phone rang, interrupting thoughts he shouldn't be thinking, he reached behind him and across the wide, antique desk to grab it. "Blue Sage," he growled into the receiver.

"Somethin' wrong there, Lucas?"

With the approaching storm, Lucas had expected to hear from his stepbrother, who lived in the foreman's house several miles away. But he'd planned on it being a discussion of the extra chores they'd be doing because of the snow. Not about his uninvited guests.

Letting his frustration at the situation get the better of him, he grunted his displeasure. "You bet somethin's wrong. I've got a woman and a boy stranded here. And there you are, enjoying yourself with your new bride."

"Did you say a woman?"

"And her boy. About six years old. Don't get any ideas. They don't belong here. They'll be nothin' but trouble. A woman is nothin' but...trouble, dammit."

Harley's heavy sigh echoed across the snowy miles. "You won't let it go, will you?" When Lucas didn't reply, he went on. "Not every woman out there is like Debra. That woman is probably nothin' like Debra. Shoot, Terri is nothin' like Deb—"

"Terri is different," Lucas snapped, turning back to stare at the inky night, propping his foot on the window seat. "I don't know how some worthless cowboy like you got yourself hooked up to that priceless female." Regretting his harsh tone, he rubbed at the back of his neck and tried to relax. "When you've been married a while longer—"

"Yeah," Harley chuckled, "she'll take off at a dead run. Or give me a house full of kids. But it won't hurt you to show a little compassion this once, Lucas. A couple of days until the storm blows on by and the roads clear. That boy and his mama don't deserve to be tossed out just because some witch of a woman did you wrong eight years ago."

Lucas didn't want to hear any of it. It was over, long over. Reminders of Debra were one thing he'd managed to avoid. The pain she'd inflicted had gone

away, and he'd been left with a hollow spot in its place
that didn't need filling.

"If I'd sent them on their way, like I should
have—"

"They'd be stranded somewhere between here and
Deerfork," Harley interjected.

"And I suppose you expect me to play white knight
and get them out of whatever trouble they're in."

"They're in trouble?"

Lucas wished he'd kept his mouth shut. "She's not
the kind to ask for help. By the look of her, the woman
has more stubborn in her than one of Zeke Chamber's
mules. I plan to stay out of it."

"But if she needs help—"

"They'll be gone in a few days. No reason to get
involved. They can go on to Great Falls as soon as the
roads are clear. Hell, I'll even give her this number,
if she runs into trouble. But other than that, I'm staying out of it."

"I'll ride over in the mornin'. I'd like to meet this
lady."

Getting Harley in the middle of this was the last
thing Lucas wanted, but after fifteen years of friendship, he knew better than to tell him not to. Doing his
best to sound unconcerned, he replied. "Suit yourself."

"What's she look like? Is she pretty?"

"I didn't notice," Lucas lied, quickly turning the
subject to ranching chores. He wasn't going to let his
partner know just how much about his guest he had
noticed or what the sound of her voice had done to
him when she'd told him her name.

They briefly discussed the extra work the storm had
caused, but all the while, Lucas listened to the sounds

of movement above him. Rachel and her son were settling in, and it looked like it would be a long night for him.

She was trouble, all right.

Chapter Two

A wan light spread into the room as Rachel opened her eyes to greet another day. It took a moment for her to remember where she was and why she was there, but for the first time in months, she felt a small measure of peace. Edward and Phyllis Harris would have a hard time finding her here. They would, eventually, somehow, but at least for a few days she could rest and gather her strength.

Dressing quickly in the clothes she'd worn the day before, she crept down the stairs and into the kitchen. With as little noise as possible, she located a can of coffee and filled the coffeemaker. As she watched the dark liquid drip into the glass carafe, she found herself mesmerized by the color, reminding her of her taciturn host.

She had expected Lucas Callahan's eyes to be as cold and hard as ice, but instead they held a warmth that had surprised her. And if she dared to be honest with herself, something in those eyes had sent a bolt of heat straight to her center. But she wasn't into daring honesty, and she shook her head, refusing to believe she'd felt anything of the kind.

With a cup of the hot brew in one hand, she moved silently, checking through the cupboards and refrigerator for breakfast supplies. She owed her host something for his hospitality. She couldn't pay him, but she could do this for him.

While sausage sizzled in a pan, pancakes cooked on a grill, and thick slices of buttered toast waited on the table, she took a quick look out the window as the sky lightened to a dull gray. To her dismay, snow continued to fall like a white curtain, shutting off the rest of the world.

Isolated. To some, the word might bring fear, but to her, it meant safety. Unless the sheriff had been suspicious and checked her license tag number, she and Cody were safe, for a few days.

The feeling of protection stayed with her as she filled several platters with food and put them on the table. Satisfied that there would be plenty to eat for a man whose job probably entailed a lot of physical labor, she started a pan of scrambled eggs.

It was ironic that she could feel so safe, staying in a house with a man who, at any moment, could endanger her future and her son's. But for some reason, she trusted Lucas Callahan. She just couldn't confide in him. She only needed a place to stay until the storm was over, and she didn't want to cause him any trouble.

Scooping the finished eggs onto a plate, she reminded herself that the longer she and Cody stayed where they were, the less money she would have to spend on a room somewhere else. Or sleep in the car, again.

She nearly dropped the plate on the table when the back door swung open with a gust of wind. Looking up, her gaze caught and held a pair of deep-brown eyes, and her breath caught in her chest. She had to get control of herself and not let merely the sight of this man affect her.

Searching her mind for something to say, Rachel stuttered on her words. ''Y-you must have a nose for food.''

Lucas's gaze slid to the table. ''Did you do this?''

Rachel nodded, not sure if he was happy to see the display of food, or angry she had made so much.

''You didn't need to,'' he said without looking at her.

She took a deep, fortifying breath, filling her lungs with much needed air and her nerves with resolve. ''I wanted to do something to thank you for letting Cody and me stay the night. I hope it was all right to raid the food supply. It looked like there's enough to last a while.''

His answer was an unconcerned shrug.

To her surprise, the door opened again. Along with another blast of frigid air, a cowboy, dressed in heavy snow gear, walked in. The moment he saw her, he removed his hat and smiled.

''Mornin'. You must be Miz Stevens.''

''Yes. Rachel Stevens.''

''Harley Peterson,'' he said, with a brief nod, and began to unfasten his coat. ''Nice to meet you, ma'am.''

''Harley's my stepbrother. He's here to help with chores,'' Lucas said from across the room.

Hope rose in her heart. "Are the roads clear?"

Harley shook his head. "I rode over from my place."

"Rode?"

"A horse."

"Oh." Her hope disappeared, and Rachel placed the eggs and the other food on the table, while tears of frustration burned her eyes. Choking back the disappointment, she set an extra place, while the cowboy peeled off his outerwear.

Unlike Lucas, Harley was big and blond, with a grin that probably made flowers grow. His sparkling blue eyes were enhanced by crinkles at the corners when he smiled, and Rachel bet her soul he smiled a lot. He was nearly as tall as Lucas, and his broad shoulders filled out the two-tone western shirt he wore. The two men were complete opposites, and so was her reaction to them.

Lucas moved across the room and flipped on a radio nestled under one of the cupboards. A Garth Brooks song filled the room. "You heard the weather report?"

"Should say somethin' soon." Harley took a chair at the table. "How's that calf?"

Rachel filled the cups with coffee and sat down, listening to the conversation. She was curious to know about ranching, but wouldn't ask for fear Lucas might think she was being nosy. It really wasn't any of her business, but since Jenny and her husband also had a small ranch, Rachel wanted to learn as much as she could before descending on them. She couldn't stay at Jenny's indefinitely, but if she could help in any way, she would. Deerfork might not offer much in the way of employment.

"I shouldn't have to call Doc Wellman about him," Lucas was saying. "He's stronger this morning."

"You'd think as big as he is, he'd be chargin' around," Harley commented around a forkful of eggs.

"Once he gets a good hold on life, he'll be the best bull of the lot."

Rachel's mind wandered as she half listened. As a little girl growing up in the foster program, going from one family to the next, she had often dreamed of escaping the busy city for a quiet spot. Jenny had been a neighbor for a short time, and they'd become best friends. When Rachel had moved on to a new family, they had kept in touch. They hadn't spoken since Steven's death, and Rachel had never mentioned the trouble with his parents. Jenny wouldn't mind a visit, but she didn't know they were on their way.

"Mom?"

Her son's voice jerked Rachel from her thoughts. "You're up early," she told him, his arms now wrapped around her legs. She quickly introduced him to Harley, then bent to ruffle his hair and kiss the top of his head. "Would you like some breakfast?"

Cody turned to look over his shoulder, never letting go of her. A sniff was followed by a hesitant nod of his head.

"There's some cereal up there in that cabinet," Harley offered. "Maybe he'd like that better."

Cody gazed up at her with an expectant look in his eyes. Disengaging herself from his hold, she gave him an encouraging pat and steered him to the empty chair. She poured out a bowl of sugared cereal and added milk, then set it in front of him. "Is that better?"

"Better." Cody's grin was visible for a split second before he dove into his breakfast.

"You ought to keep him off those sweets," Lucas announced.

Stung, Rachel stared at him. She was a good mother, but kids just liked sweet cereal over a conventional breakfast. If they had been at home, she might have insisted that Cody eat something more nutritious, or at least add a glass of juice. But they weren't at home, and Cody deserved a treat.

"And how many children do you have, Mr. Callahan?" she asked in a wounded voice.

"None," Lucas snapped back.

She could have sworn she saw a flash of pain in his eyes before he turned his attention to his plate. The man hadn't said a word to Cody since they had arrived except to ask his name.

"I was thinkin' of the boy." He looked pointedly at her and then at Cody.

Embarrassment and traces of anger heated her cheeks. Staying here was a mistake, but not one she could do anything about. As long as no one knew her true identity, she and Cody would be safe. For a while.

Lucas knew she was lying. He watched her leave the table, the uncertainty of her steps adding to his conviction. It hadn't taken him long to know that she couldn't be involved in a burglary ring. One look in her eyes the night before had told him that much. Whatever she was hiding from had her running scared. A part of him, buried for so many years, wanted to shield her from whatever her troubles might be. But the other part told him her troubles would be his if he didn't watch it. With a sixth sense, he knew they wouldn't be something he would want to get involved with. If he wasn't careful, he'd be smack in the middle of it before long. He could only hope the weather cleared, and she and the boy could be on their way.

While they finished breakfast, she kept busy. His gaze slid over her slender body as she turned on the faucet and started running a sink full of soapy water. Her jeans stretched tight across her hips and bottom, causing his mouth to go dry. He'd dare anyone to guess she had carried a child with hips that slim. The thought crossed his mind that the boy might not be hers, but after a glance at Cody, he knew better. The youngster might not have those same blue eyes, but the mouth was wide and full like hers.

Reminding himself that women, slim-hipped or full-hipped, were nothing but trouble, he watched her for a reaction to his next question. "You have out-of-state plates. Where are you from?"

She stiffened slightly, and her hand, reaching for the griddle on the stove, stopped midway. "Ohio," she answered. "Cincinnati, to be exact." She grabbed the pan and plopped it into the water. "We have snow there, too."

"Not like this, I'll bet," he thought out loud.

She turned, offering him a weak smile. "No, nothing like this. And not nearly so early in the year. I never expected anything like this."

He could see that much was the truth. "Early for here, too. First measurable snowfall usually isn't until later in September."

"Does that mean more work with the animals?" she asked, her back to them once again.

"We'll have to take some hay bales out to the herd."

"Is it a large herd?" Rachel asked.

"Large enough to keep us busy," Lucas answered,

his long-sleeping hormones awakening. Every time she scrubbed at the pan she was washing, her hips swayed from side to side. He wanted to tell her to put the damn pan down. He wanted to grab her and turn her around, look into her eyes, and demand she tell him the truth.

Only he didn't want to know the truth, he reminded himself.

"Jenny and Pete have cattle," she said, as if to herself.

"Different breed."

"I thought cows were cows," she quipped over her shoulder with a grin.

"Do you know anything about cattle?" Lucas questioned her.

"Only that they're raised and sold for meat and sometimes leather," she answered. "And they moo," she added with a laugh.

"And milk, Mom," Cody reminded her.

She dried her hands and approached the table. "And milk," she agreed, picking up his empty bowl.

Lucas watched her comb Cody's hair with her long, tapered fingers and imagined how they'd feel skimming through his own hair. "Hell," he muttered, shoving away from the table.

"What?" she asked, looking over her shoulder at him.

"Are those the only clothes you have?" he answered with a question of his own. *And what do you look like without them?* He swallowed the groan that nearly escaped him at the picture in his mind.

She looked down and picked at the hem of her shirt. "They're still in the car," she said before looking up at him. "I didn't want to put you to any more trouble."

If she knew how much trouble she was causing him, Lucas was sure she'd head for the hills. Hell, he hadn't had insane thoughts that verged on lewd for years. He'd had enough women since his ex-wife to keep him at least close to satisfied. Women who filled his hands much more than this one would. But still, there was something about her....

He stuffed his hands in his pockets at the thought of touching her. "I'll get them."

"No!" she blurted. "I mean, I'll just go out and get what we'll need for another day."

"You can't be traipsin' out in those flimsy shoes." He looked down at her thin canvas shoes and noticed how small her feet were. "You'd end up with frostbite."

Her chin went up and her eyes flashed with defiance. "A little snow and cold isn't going to hurt me. Cody has a snowsuit out there, and boots and mittens."

"Mittens?"

"He's only six," she snapped.

"Aren't six-year-old boys usually in school?"

Cody answered the question. "I'm in school back home. Mom says this is a special vacation."

"Vacation?" Lucas nailed her with a look, waiting for an answer.

"Let's get their clothes, Lucas," Harley said from the door.

Lucas held her fearful gaze with a promise in his own that they weren't finished. Without a word, he joined Harley, grabbed his coat and hat, and pulled the door open.

"You're pushin' too hard," Harley told him once they were outside.

"Maybe." Wet snow hit him full in the face and the wind nearly sent his hat flying.

"I thought you didn't want any part of it?" Harley reminded him.

They braced themselves against the wind, and Lucas saved his answer until they were inside the shed where he had parked her car. He waited while Harley took the keys from the ignition and returned to the back of the car. "That's what I said. Maybe I was wrong."

"Wrong?" Harley's hand stilled on the key in the trunk lock, and a slow grin crept over his face. "You, Lucas? That'd be a first, wouldn't it?"

"Just get it open," Lucas growled.

With a flick of his wrist, Harley opened the trunk and stared inside. "All this for a vacation?"

Cardboard boxes sealed with tape were stuffed between a set of expensive luggage. Toys were crammed in every spare inch, along with more shoes than most people would wear in a month.

"Hell," Lucas muttered.

"She's runnin'."

"Yep."

Harley pulled two suitcases out and handed them to Lucas, then turned back for the other two. "Think we ought to mention it?"

"Nope." Lucas considered the collection of belongings. "But I think we ought to keep an eye on her. Give me the keys."

"Now, Lucas—"

He held out his hand. "Give me the keys, Harley. I don't want her running off before we can find out what's happening."

Harley hesitated. "You're going to help her?"

"I'm going to find out what's going on and make sure she's not on the wrong side of trouble. That's all. I won't say anything to Ben unless I think it's important."

Harley passed him the set of keys. "Then let me ask the questions. You're about as subtle as a runaway freight train."

Lucas picked up the two bags. "You always were better with women."

Harley's laughter echoed in the old building. "Me? Hell, Lucas, they always flocked to you like flies to an outhouse."

Lucas ignored the jab and started out into the weather. "I'll do the asking. I'll find out what her name really is and have Ben check it out."

"You don't think it's Rachel Stevens?"

"If it is, mine is Satan."

"Did I say something wrong, Mom?" Cody asked when the two men were gone.

Rachel had some explaining to do about her little white lies. But this wasn't the time. "No, it's all right, honey. Why don't you run upstairs and get your books out of the backpack? You can look at the pictures while I clean up. I'll read it to you later."

"Can I try to read it?"

Pride filled her heart. Cody had been able to read since kindergarten, far ahead of the other students in his class. "Sure you can."

"Yippee!" he shouted as he ran out of the room.

With a sigh, she picked up the empty plates from the table and put them in the sink. The men would be back soon, and she'd have to answer some questions.

She had hoped to put it off for a while longer. But just how little could she get away with telling Lucas? She owed him some kind of explanation. And now she was forced to tell the truth. To a point.

The last fork dropped in the drawer with a clatter when the door opened behind her. Bracing herself for more questions, she turned to see the snow-covered cowboys enter, carrying her four suitcases.

"We'll put them up in the bedroom," Harley told her as they passed through the room.

She breathed a sigh of relief when Lucas didn't bother to look her way. She watched him walk out, the muscles in his back and shoulders bunching at the weight of the luggage in his hands. Her knees wobbled beneath her, and her heartbeat quickened. She still stared when he was no longer in sight.

Get a grip, Rache. She had seen men with well-toned bodies before. *Well-toned?* Okay, she relented. Hunky bodies. But none that kept her eyes glued to them and made her heart pound. There hadn't been a man yet who could catch her attention and hold it for more than five minutes, especially after she'd found out how most of them were like Steven. And she had a feeling Lucas Callahan was more like Steven than all of them.

With a muttered reminder to keep her lusting thoughts under control, she started for the hallway and the stairs, only to find herself nose to chest with her cold host. Her heart leapt to her throat, and she silently cursed her reaction.

"I—I was just going to check on Cody," she murmured, looking up. She instantly wished she hadn't. Eyes like two pieces of burning coal gazed down into hers.

"He's talkin' to Harley."

His voice slid over her like warm honey on a hot biscuit and left her speechless.

"Rachel Stevens, right?"

She could only nod.

One corner of his mouth lifted in a smile that resembled a smirk. "That's what I thought," he said and moved past her.

She grabbed the banister for support. Lordy, if the man had horns and a forked tail, he'd be the spitting image of Lucifer, fire in his eyes and all.

With a quick look over her shoulder to make sure he had gone, she let the moan slide through her lips. She needed a swift kick in the rear, that's what she needed.

You need a man, a voice whispered in her mind.

"That's not likely," she answered out loud.

"Who are you talking to, Mom?" Cody asked from above her.

Rachel looked up and forced a smile to her lips. Hoping her shaking knees would carry her, she climbed the stairs. "Just myself. I'm a great conversationalist. What are you and Harley doing up there?"

At the top of the stairs, Cody grabbed her hand and pulled her down the hallway to the room they'd shared the night before. "I was showing him how good I can read. He gave me some books."

"That's nice of him," she replied, shaking the mental image of Lucas from her mind.

"You've got a smart boy there," Harley said, when she stepped into the room. "I thought Cody might like to look at these. I've been storin' stuff here since Lucas and I were teenagers." He knelt beside a box on the floor, opened it, and pulled out a stout pile of children's books. "Some of these belong to Lucas, but he won't mind."

"He might," Rachel muttered.

Harley looked up at her, his eyes troubled, before turning back to Cody. "Why don't we sit in that big chair over there? I bet you can't read three of them to me in the next thirty minutes."

"Bet I can," Cody challenged, scrambling into the chair with an armload of books and making room for the big man.

"Lucas wants to see you down in the living room," Harley told her, then settled next to her son.

Rachel held her breath, knowing the questions were going to start. It would be difficult, without giving too much away, but she'd have to answer.

Cody dragged his attention from the open book in his hands and looked up. "Where's the living room?"

"Bottom of the stairs and turn right," Harley answered.

Obviously enthralled with his bounty, Cody snuggled in deeper and began reading. It brought a smile to Rachel's lips, but it didn't last long.

Remembering the directions, she left the room and took the stairs slowly, gathering her courage. At the bottom, she turned right and entered the living room. After a quick glance around, she took a deep breath and faced Lucas. "Did you want to talk to me about something?"

"I have some questions," he said without looking at her.

She knew her best defense was to play dumb. "About what?"

"There's a lot of boxes in your trunk. It looks like you and Cody are on more than a vacation."

"I have some things to take to Jenny," she fibbed.

His gaze swiveled to hers and held her. "You're planning to stay there for a while?"

"I'm not sure how long we'll be there," she offered. "Jenny and I haven't seen each other for years."

"Have you talked to her?"

"Not—not recently, but yes, we've talked."

"From Cincinnati?"

She swallowed the fear that rose in her throat. She never should have told him that. She and Cody had lived there for a short while, but only long enough to prove residency and get an Ohio license and her car tagged. Edward and Phyllis weren't far behind them there, and they'd left as soon as they had enough money. Jenny didn't have a clue they'd ever been there.

"Yes, from Cincinnati."

"So if Jenny or Pete should call, and I tell them that her friend from Cincinnati is here, they'll know who I'm talking about?"

Her pounding heart plummeted to a thud in her stomach. "No," she whispered.

"I didn't think so," he said, his voice low. "Maybe you'd better sit down."

Other than escaping, nothing sounded quite so good. Knees shaking, Rachel sank onto the nearest chair. Lucas sat on the chair across from her and waited.

"Mr. Callahan," she began, attempting to still her spinning thoughts, "I'm not doing anything wrong, if that's what you're thinking."

"Nobody said you were."

Nodding, she absorbed the sliver of good news. "But you suspect I might be."

"I'm concerned, is all."

She choked back her laugh. Concerned? She'd been telling a few white lies, but this was a whopper. "There's no need for you to be concerned," she assured him. "We'll be out of your house as soon as possible. We wouldn't even be here if it weren't for the snowstorm."

"That's what worries me."

She got to her feet. "It's not your job to worry about us." Giving it a second thought, she said the only thing she could. "I don't want you involved in this. The less you know, the better off we'll all be."

"And Jen will be safe?" He shook his head. "Doesn't make sense."

Searching her mind for something to dissuade him from asking more, she paced the room.

"Come on, Rachel, or whatever your name is." He frowned, then cocked one black eyebrow at her. "What is your name, anyway?"

"Rachel Stevens."

"Try again."

She shook her head. "My name is Rachel."

Shoving out of the chair, he nodded. He walked across the room to her and stopped in front of her. "I'll have to take you at your word. But you need to remember one thing. I'm not much for lies. Or secrets."

When he'd gone, leaving her alone and shaking, she sank back onto the chair. It had been as bad as she'd expected. No, it had been worse. He'd been so close, she had felt the heat radiating from his body, seen his chest rise and fall, with each breath he took. Like the earlier episode on the stairs, she had nearly lost control of herself.

But she hadn't. She couldn't. For some reason she couldn't identify, Lucas Callahan did things to her by simply walking into a room, that no man ever had. It was wrong. She was nothing more than an accidental guest, and her visit would only be for a few days. She wasn't the type of woman who could have a brief fling, and he wasn't the type of man who would want anything more. If he even wanted that. He'd given no indication that he did.

She couldn't blame him for asking questions, but she couldn't give him any more information. It wasn't just for her sake and Cody's. Lucas would be much better off not knowing.

His parting words drifted back to her, and she knew this wouldn't be the last time he would question her. She could only pray that she and Cody could leave within a day or two. She didn't like to lie, but her secret must be kept.

In the silence of the room, she whispered, "But Lucas has his own secrets, I'll bet."

Chapter Three

A smile curved Lucas's lips as he stood outside the closed living room door, but it was quickly replaced by a worried frown. He'd gotten just enough information to worry him.

Rachel. The name fit her. Soft and warm, yet there was strength in it. Like the strength he saw in her. He still suspected her last name wasn't Stevens. The woman was a walking pack of lies. But he had a feeling she didn't like telling them any more than he liked hearing them.

As he made his way to his office, he replayed their conversation in his mind. She had done a fine job of avoiding his questions. He hadn't liked doing it. All the time he was asking, he'd felt like an interrogator. But he needed answers, if nothing more than out of simple curiosity. Only it was more than that. As much as he'd grown to distrust women, there was something about this particular one that kept tugging at him. It was nothing she said. In fact, he sensed her drawing

away from him, whenever he was around. He suspected it was her way of protecting herself. She didn't
trust him. He couldn't blame her for that. If she had
caught even a hint of what he'd been thinking and
feeling around her, she had good reason. He didn't
trust himself.

When the door opened, he looked up to see his stepbrother. Harley glanced into the hallway, then shut the
door behind him. "How'd it go?"

Lucas didn't want to admit how much it had bothered him to question her. "Fine, but I didn't learn a
lot. It might be easier to find out something from
Cody."

Harley's head moved back and forth. "I don't
know, Lucas. He's only six." A grin replaced his
frown. "But he's smart as a whip. He can read as good
as a kid twice his age."

Lucas barely noted the comment. The boy reminded
him too much of what he'd lost. "Maybe you should
talk to him. Find out what you can. He doesn't think
much of me."

Harley settled into his favorite chair. "I think you
scare him, Lucas."

"Scare him? I've hardly said a word to him."

"Try smilin' once in a while," Harley suggested.
"I think you even scare Rachel."

She ought to be scared. Lucas had to admit to himself that his own reaction to her scared him. He'd managed to keep his distance. Except for that little meeting
on the stairs. Because of that, he'd escaped to the office with his teeth gritted so hard to keep from pulling
her up next to him, his jaws hurt. The scent of peaches
had been all over her. Sweet, succulent peaches. A
rarity on the ranch, especially in the winter months.

The aroma had made his dry mouth water with the need to see if she tasted the same. Just one kiss, one taste, and he could have his answer and forget—

"...Marty and John gonna get here?"

Lucas jerked his thoughts back to the business at hand, glad Harley couldn't read his mind. "John said he'd talked to Marty." He glanced at his watch. "They ought to be here about dinnertime. You don't think...?"

"Bet she would," Harley answered the unfinished question with a grin.

Lucas got to his feet. "Good. You can ask her."

"Oh, no," Harley argued. He stood, stopping Lucas on his way to the door. "I'm takin' Cody outside. You ask her."

Lucas shook his head. He didn't want to be alone in the same room with her, if he could help it. God only knew what he might do. He needed time to get himself under control. "She'll refuse if I ask."

"Oh, hell, Lucas," Harley laughed. "Use some of that Callahan charm on her."

Lucas considered it. He could keep it brief. He'd ask, she'd answer, and he'd be out the door. She would either rustle up a dinner for them all, or they'd scrounge for whatever they could throw together. He'd just keep some distance from her.

"You want me to cook for six people?" Rachel asked when Lucas approached her.

Hell, all she had to do was say yes or no. He kept his distance, but it didn't seem to help much. Even from across the room, he could smell peaches. Or imagined he did. "There's plenty of stuff here," he pointed out.

Her teeth sunk into her bottom lip, nearly bringing a groan from him. She shook her head and muttered, "I don't know what I can fix."

He waited for his chance to escape. "Fix anything," he snapped. "John and Marty will be so hungry when they get here, they won't take time to notice what it is."

She walked to the cabinet, reached up and opened it wide. Lucas closed his eyes and took a deep breath. She'd changed into another pair of jeans, and dammit if they weren't tighter than the others. She had exchanged the oversize sweatshirt for a shirt that hugged her close and barely grazed the tops of her pockets. Until she stretched up to reach high into the cabinet. With the simple movement, she bared a large expanse of creamy skin above the waistband of her jeans.

He couldn't stop his feet from moving him toward her, his gaze riveted on her flesh. Before he reached touching distance, she turned her head to glance back.

"I—" She stopped, staring at him, her blue eyes wide. Her arms dropped to her sides, and she tugged at the bottom of her shirt, pulling it down. Her cheeks turned a rosy shade of pink. "I'll find something. I'll get Cody to help."

"I promised to show him around the ranch," Lucas managed to say without choking. He had to get out before he did something they would both regret. Concentrating on keeping his feet from tangling with each other, he started backing up.

"He needs his snowsuit and—"

"He's got it," Lucas barked. "You think a man doesn't know how to dress a little kid?"

"Of course," she whispered. Her eyes glittered, and her teeth scraped her lip again.

He yanked on his coat, then grabbed behind his back for the doorknob, missed it, and swore under his breath. His second try brought success, and he was out the door so fast, he closed it on the brim of his hat.

"Hey, Lucas!" Harley called to him from the corral. "Come give us a hand."

Shaking his head to clear the fog, Lucas clomped through the snow. In the corral, Harley had tied an aged sled behind their oldest, slowest horse. Cody sat on the sled, gripping the sides.

"Hey, Cody, you warm enough?" Lucas hollered.

Cody's head bobbed up and down, and he stared at Lucas.

Lucas strode through the snow to tug the little boy's knit cap farther onto his head. "Your mom is worried about you."

Cody shrank away from him. "I'm okay. 'S not c-cold."

Yeah, sure. Even Lucas could feel the bite of the wind. He looked up to see a silly grin on Harley's face. "What?"

Harley's grin widened.

"Harley, what the—"

"Smile," Harley replied, then ducked behind Bay Roller.

"Oh, yeah," Lucas mumbled. Attempting his widest smile, he hunkered down by Cody. "You ever been sleddin'?"

Cody's head swiveled from side to side.

"It's been a long time for me, too," he admitted. "Now, you hang on tight."

Harley handed him the halter rope. "I'll get started on the rest of the chores. Go easy with him."

Lucas shot him a glare. Didn't anyone trust him with Cody? "I can handle it."

"I mean about the questions."

Lucas wondered just how to go about questioning a six-year-old. The idea wasn't something he was comfortable with, but it had to be done. "I will," he called, as Harley walked away.

He urged the old horse forward, watching the sled, ready to catch Cody if he toppled off. But Cody hung on tight, laughing with delight, while he led Bay Roller faster around the corral.

"That was fun," Cody told Lucas as they untied the rope and led Bay Roller into the barn. "Can we do it again sometime?"

"As long as the snow sticks around," Lucas promised. He looked down into a pair of sparkling hazel eyes and felt a pang of unease. Cody slipped his small hand into Lucas's big one, and Lucas nearly jerked away. But once he realized the boy finally trusted him, his heart beat with a new warmth, and a real smile eased onto his face.

The old stove at the far end of the barn crackled and burned brightly. "Strip off your snow gear," he directed.

While Cody complied, he undid his own coat and retrieved a bag of marshmallows Harley had left. "You won't believe this." he announced.

"Oh, boy!" Cody jumped up and down, his snowsuit bunched around his knees, half on and half off. "Are we going to roast them?"

Lucas produced a tin of hot cocoa mix. "I thought they'd go good with this."

It didn't take long for them to find themselves enjoying the warmth of the old stove, each with a hot cup of cocoa in their hands, topped with fat marsh-mallows.

Cody looked up at Lucas, his eyebrows drawn to-gether in a frown. "I didn't know cowboys drank hot chocolate."

"Sure we do. I've been doing this since I was your size. Can't let a good snowstorm pass without it."

"Really?"

Lucas wiped at the marshmallow smudge above Cody's upper lip and winked at him. "Yeah, really. Sometimes I stay out here for days and days."

"I bet my daddy never did anything like this," Cody said in a quiet voice.

"Where is your daddy?" Something had a tight grip on his chest. Hell, he'd never given a thought to Ra-chel having a husband. It made sense that she might be running from a husband. What a fool he'd been to lust after her, when he didn't know anything about her.

"He's in heaven," Cody answered with a shrug of one shoulder. "At least that's what my mom told me."

A long, slow breath of air eased out of Lucas. He thought of his own father, a man who'd deserted his family. His memories weren't happy ones. "Did you like living in Ohio?" he asked to change the subject.

"We didn't live there very long," Cody replied. "We lived in Chicago before that. And I went to kin-dergarten in Detroit."

"You've done some traveling."

"Yeah," Cody answered. "But you know what? I like it better here than anywhere. Mom says we might stay for a long time. Do you think Jenny will let me visit you when it snows again?"

"Any time your mom says it's okay," Lucas told him. It surprised him to find that he liked the idea. Jen and Pete didn't live far. He would have a chance to see Cody. And Rachel.

He got to his feet, stretching out the kinks as he gathered the empty cups. He grabbed a blanket and bundled it around Cody. "Your snow gear's still wet," he explained when the boy started to protest.

Carrying Cody to the house, Lucas brought up the subject of Rachel's dead husband, while he still had the chance to ask. "Cody, what was your daddy's name?"

"Steven," the boy answered on a yawn. "Gramma Harris said he was too young to die."

Steven Stevens? "Is that your mom's mama?" he asked Cody.

Cody's eyelids fluttered shut, and he yawned. "No. She's my daddy's mom. My mom doesn't have a mom."

So Grandma Harris was Rachel's mother-in-law. That meant—

Rachel Harris. Now Lucas had a name. Ben could run a check on her, and maybe they could find out what kind of trouble she was in. Not that Lucas wanted to help her. He just needed to know the truth. But exactly why, he didn't want to think about.

While the house was empty, Rachel took the opportunity to do a little picking up. Men, she'd learned long ago, didn't know how to pick up after themselves. She had tried to teach Cody, but she often wondered if there wasn't a gene missing in the male physiology.

She put a pot of simple hamburger stew to simmer on the stove and got busy. Hoping Lucas wouldn't mind her doing a little laundry, she'd tossed a load of

hers and Cody's clothes in the washing machine. She
had been in too big of a hurry for several days to stop,
and their supply of clean clothes was running low.
Cody's especially. She could name every meal they'd
had just by looking at the front of his shirts.

She had noticed papers scattered on the countertops
in the kitchen and gathered them into neat stacks, sort-
ing between newspapers and cattle sale flyers and
magazines. Making a circle of the lower floor of the
house, she picked up a variety of clothing and other
belongings. She sorted through the clothes, planning
to do another load of wash, and left them in a pile
near the foot of the stairs. Finding the stash of cleaning
supplies, she grabbed a dust cloth and went over the
furniture before plugging in the vacuum to do the car-
pets. She wondered how long it had been since anyone
had given the place a good, thorough cleaning.

As she vacuumed the hallway, she passed the door
to a room she immediately recognized as an office.
The desk was piled high with papers and open books
that had obviously come from the wide bookcase
stretching along one wall. Empty coffee cups littered
the room, along with crumpled balls of paper that had
missed the trash container by several feet.

Leaving the vacuum running to do a little straightening, she picked up the debris on the floor and started
to gather the books that lay scattered among it. Un-
derneath a thick volume of veterinary information, she
found a large, leather album. Tired of cleaning and in
need of a short rest, she sat on a chair by the desk and
placed the album in front of her, curiosity getting the
better of her.

She opened the cover to find a page of old pictures.
Most of them were of a man and a woman smiling

into the camera, their arms around each other. The
man bore a strong resemblance to Lucas, although he
wasn't nearly as dark and dangerous looking. The
woman was slight, with dark eyes alight with love and
happiness. A heavy mane of hair surrounded her face
like a dark, glowing halo.

On the next page, the woman held a baby, her smile
soft as she looked down at the tiny infant in her arms.
There was no doubt in Rachel's mind that the couple
was Lucas's parents. When she turned the page again,
she found a newspaper clipping, announcing the birth
of a son, Lucas, to Raymond and Marie Claire Callahan, confirming her deduction.

Amid snapshots of ranch activities, a little boy's
birthday parties and others, various newspaper clippings had been taped. As she read, she learned that
Lucas's father had been a bronc rider in the rodeo.
Looking farther through the book, she noticed that the
clippings and pictures of the man ceased to be among
those of the boy and his mother. When she came to a
picture of four people, she recognized three of them.
Lucas, his mother, and a blond boy dressed in a cowboy shirt that matched Lucas's. Harley. The big man
standing with them was obviously Harley's father.
With his arm around Marie Claire, Rachel wondered
what had happened to Lucas's father.

Several more pages into the book, she stopped, staring at the glossy picture before her. Lucas, dressed in
a tuxedo, stood with a beautiful woman in a long,
white, wedding dress and veil. Candles glowed in the
background. Turning the page with trembling fingers,
she found another photo of the pair with Harley posing
with them. The light in Lucas's eyes as he gazed down
at his bride brought a lump to her throat. He obviously

adored the woman. Where was she now? Had Lucas lost his wife, the same as she'd lost Steven? That would explain his constant frown.

"What the hell do you think you're doing?" Lucas's voice boomed from behind her.

Rachel jerked back in the chair and turned to look at him, feeling suddenly ashamed for snooping. "I— I was just picking things up."

Lucas flipped off the noisy vacuum and faced her. His black hat shadowed the top of his face, but Rachel could see the deep frown drawing down his mouth. With his hands balled into fists at his side, he crossed the room in three long strides.

"Where did you find that?" he thundered at her.

From her vantage point, she could look up and see his eyes under the brim of his hat. Hard and cold, like pieces of coal, they stared into her. She commanded her galloping heart to slow and gathered her wits before speaking. "I'm sorry. I didn't mean to pry. I found it on the floor."

"So now you know everything about me?" he asked, a bitter smile twisting his lips.

She pulled her gaze from his and looked down at the smiling couple in the photo. "Only that you're married."

"*Was* married," he corrected in a hard voice.

"I'm sorry." She stared at her hands for a moment, then raised her gaze to his. Her heart went out to this man, who obviously still carried a lot of pain. "Is she…gone?"

His harsh laugh sent a chill through her. "She's gone, all right."

Swallowing the lump in her throat, she dared to ask, "Did she…die?"

"Die?" He laughed again. "She should have. It would have been better for all of us if she had."

Rachel couldn't believe what she was hearing. She'd seen bitterness before. Growing up in foster homes and living in big cities, she'd seen more than enough to recognize it. But it was the icy loathing in his eyes that hit her the hardest.

Shoving the book away, she stood. "That's a horrid thing to say."

He grabbed her, his fingers biting into her arms. Too scared to move, she looked up at him. His dark eyes flashed fire at her. "Is it?" he demanded. His gaze slid to the album on the desk. "You didn't know her. If you had, you'd think differently."

"Nobody deserves to be talked about that way," she dared to say.

He turned back to her, his eyes still cold. But when they met her gaze, the frigid flame warmed. One hand reached to stroke her cheek. "Rachel..."

His rough whisper sent tingles racing along her nerve endings. Her lips parted on a soft gasp at the new sensation, and he inched closer.

"Hey, Mom! There's two cowboys outside on horses!"

Lucas released her as if he'd been burned, nearly dumping her into the chair behind her.

"Th-that's great, Cody," she stammered. Pressing her fingers to her temples, she took a deep breath and stumbled over the chair to get to the door. Her heart thundered in her ears, and she could feel the heat on her face. And the heat he'd awakened within her frightened her. "I bet they're hungry, too," she added as she rushed from the room.

* * *

"Damn!" Lucas slammed his fist on the desk only to find he'd landed it in the middle of his wedding picture. "Damn!"

"John and Marty are here," Harley announced from the open doorway.

Lucas nodded, his throat too thick with disgust of himself to speak. Clearing it, he closed the album and held it out to Harley. "What is this doing out?" he demanded.

Harley took the book from him and stuck it under his arm. "Last time I remember, we were looking through it for the name of that stock company down in Laramie. Maybe we didn't put it up."

"Just get it out of here." Lucas turned and braced his hands on the edge of the desk, hanging his head.

"How much did she see?" Harley asked from behind him.

Without turning, Lucas answered. "Enough to ask a couple of questions."

"Like what?"

Lucas didn't answer immediately. "She asked if Debra had died."

"What'd you tell her?"

"I told her it was too bad she hadn't," Lucas admitted with a dry laugh. "Rachel didn't take too kindly to it."

"Nope, I guess she wouldn't." The sound of Harley moving to the door cut into the silence. "Dinner's on the table. Marty and John are fallin' all over themselves tryin' to help."

"Are they, now?" Lucas grumbled. He straightened and turned to Harley. "I'll be there in a minute. Tell Rachel—tell her not to hold up dinner. I've got a couple of things to do."

Harley nodded before walking out, leaving Lucas to unscramble his emotions. He shouldn't have reacted so violently when he saw Rachel with the old photo album. But the thing brought back memories he had buried long ago. He didn't need them dug up again. Debra had left a bad taste in a lot of people's mouths. But it was nothing compared to what she had left him with.

His ex-wife had given him a twisted and obscene view of just how bad a female could be, souring him on all women. Over the years, he'd tried to tell himself they weren't all like her. In fact, he knew some of them weren't. But other than Marie Claire, his mother, and Harley's wife, Terri, he hadn't met many. And the ones he had met had already found better men than he. Men who could let down their guard. Lucas could never do that. Distrust was as much a part of him as breathing. Nothing could change that.

Hardening himself to his own reality, Lucas went to dinner, resolved to apologize to Rachel later for laying a hand on her. It had been an insane action. He hadn't meant to do it. But the soft, sad look in her eyes had touched a part of his heart he'd thought had died. He could only silently thank Cody for bursting in before anything else happened.

He entered the kitchen, and the sight before him brought him to a halt. Standing in the doorway, he had a clear view of his two hired hands making fools of themselves over Rachel.

"This is the best meal I've ever had," Marty announced with a goofy grin directed at her.

Her answering smile made Lucas's blood run hot and then cold. He froze when she winked at Marty. "I'll bet you say that to all the cooks," she teased.

"Just the female ones," John quipped. "But I don't believe I've ever had anything that tasted this good."

Both of them! Lucas marched to his chair, determined to put a stop to the display of foolishness. A quick glance at Rachel told him she was avoiding looking at him. "You boys ready to put in some hard work?"

"Soon as all this food is gone," John answered. Lucas nearly groaned at the look of lust in the man's eyes when he looked at Rachel. "Where you been keepin' her, Lucas?"

"I haven't been *keepin'* her anywhere," Lucas snarled from between clenched teeth. He saw the look Harley gave him and tried to smile. It hurt.

"She hasn't even been here twenty-four hours," Harley reminded with a chuckle. "She made it in last night just before the storm hit. I told you both that."

"You can get snowed in at my place anytime," John told her, a suggestive twinkle in his eyes. "It's a lot smaller than this place, but cozier."

Rachel's smile wavered, and her cheeks pinked when she glanced at Lucas. "It's cozy enough here, thank you, John."

Marty offered up his coffee cup when she lifted the pot. "How long are you goin' to be here?" he asked, his eyes never straying from her.

"I'll be leaving as soon as my tire is repaired and the snow clears," Rachel said with determination.

Marty and John groaned in protest.

"The Blue Sage could sure use a good cook," John tempted. "And I'll bet Lou could use some help at The Rusty Dog. Marty and me would make eatin' there a habit, if we knew you were there."

Lucas had to force himself to stay in his seat.

"The Rusty Dog?" Rachel asked with interest. "Is that in Deerfork?"

Marty grinned across the table. "Yep. Part café, part saloon. Lou barbecues the best ribs in the county."

Rachel's eyes lit up. "And you think this Lou might be needing some help?"

Lucas decided to put a halt to the idea. "You don't want to work at Lou's. Too many rowdy cowboys."

"Oh, I can handle rowdy cowboys," Rachel said with a wide grin and a glance around the table.

Lucas stared at her, imagining Rachel sashaying through The Rusty Dog while every male in the place made passes at her. He bit back a groan and cleared his throat. "Let's get goin' boys," he announced, standing.

"But—" Marty began.

Lucas nailed him with a frown. "There's work to do. Let's get to it."

The hands, including Harley, mumbled in protest, but pushed away from the table and stood. Harley was the first to the door and grabbed his coat and hat. "Lucas is right. Sooner we get to it, sooner we'll be done for the day, and I can get home to my wife."

"Can I go, too, Mom?"

Lucas swung around to see Cody. The boy had been so quiet, and Lucas had been so intent on watching the men and Rachel, he hadn't noticed the boy.

He pulled Cody's coat from the rack. "He can ride with me."

Uncertainty shone in Rachel's eyes. She looked from Cody to Lucas. "I don't know...."

"It's warmed up some," Lucas offered. "And the wind's stopped blowing. If he gets cold, I'll bring him back."

"Well…"

"Please, Mom?"

Rachel hesitated before sliding a glance at Lucas, then gave Cody a soft smile. "All right. For a while. But if you get cold, you let Lucas know. I can't affor—" She stopped, shaking her head. "I don't want you getting sick. Okay?"

Cody had already jumped from his chair and was shrugging into the coat Lucas held for him. "Okay, I promise."

Lucas knew the boys could do most of the feeding, and they wouldn't be out long. He and Harley could check fences another time, although time spent away from the house was what he needed most. He followed the others to the door and was reaching for the knob when Rachel stopped him.

"Lucas?"

He swallowed the tension that being in the same room with her caused and turned.

"You didn't eat much. Is—" she lowered her head "—is my cooking that bad?"

He felt about as big as a tick on a dog's belly. He hadn't had anything that good, except for Lou's ribs, since before his mother had died. But he couldn't find his voice. "Not hungry," he managed to reply.

She raised her head to look at him, and their gazes caught and held. "I'll put the leftovers in the—the refrigerator in case you are later."

"Much obliged." It took every bit of control he had to look away. Grabbing his hat, he stuffed it on his head and bolted out the door.

"Hell," he muttered on the porch. He had to put a lid on this…whatever it was. He felt like a randy teenager around her. And it wasn't good. Not at all. Not for either of them.

Chapter Four

Rachel collapsed onto the nearest kitchen chair and let out the breath she had been holding, relieved to finally be alone. She'd hardly had time to think about the encounter in the office. What had come over her? What was happening? She raised her hand to her cheek, remembering Lucas's touch and the tenderness she had seen in his eyes. It was the complete opposite of the man who'd walked into the ranch office, scaring her to death. She'd wanted to run and hide. Until he touched her. He had set her body on fire. If Cody hadn't burst in…

Shoving her rampaging thoughts aside, she stood and busied herself with clearing the table. She filled the sink with hot, soapy water and plunged her hands into it, scrubbing furiously at the plates while she chastised herself for being a fool. Lucas Callahan was a hard, cold man. She couldn't let herself think otherwise. So what if he made her pulse race and her knees weak? She would do better to remember that he was a man who held his ex-wife in contempt, not someone who could attract her the way he was doing. She needed to get away, not only for herself, but for her son. Cody was growing too fond of the rancher. Once Jenny and Pete returned, she wanted her son to forget about the friends he'd made at the Blue Sage Ranch. She doubted he would. She had hated taking him away from his friends each time they'd had to leave, but if she had to keep running with him, she would.

While she waited for the men to return, she made plans. She sat at the table with a piece of paper and the stub of a pencil, jotting down every possible place she could wait for Jenny's return. It kept her mind from drifting to a dark-eyed cowboy, but even that took some effort. She was deep in thought when the door opened and Harley walked in, carrying a sleeping Cody.

"All that fresh air tuckered him out," Harley said with a grin. "I'll just go put him up in his bed."

She laid her hand on his arm to stop him. "Thank you."

The door opened again, and she turned to look. Lucas stepped inside, kicking the door closed behind him. He reached for his hat, but his hand stopped midway when his gaze narrowed on where she was touching Harley.

Snatching her hand away, she tucked it behind her. "Maybe I should take Cody upstairs."

Harley glanced over his shoulder at Lucas, who had removed his hat. "Don't want to wake him," he told Rachel. "It'll only take a minute."

She watched him carry her son out of the room and took a deep breath. The silence in the big kitchen seemed to crowd at her senses. She moved to the refrigerator. "Would you like those leftovers now?" she asked without looking back.

Lucas didn't answer, at first. When he did, his voice sounded strained. "Maybe later."

She couldn't turn around, couldn't face him. Not knowing what else to do, she reached for the dish towel and refolded it as slowly as she could. Her nerves were stretched tight. She could feel him watching her, and a slow warmth crept through her body.

He cleared his throat. "About what happened earlier—"

"Forget it," she snapped. She closed her eyes at the sharp sound of her own voice. She hadn't meant to be rude, she only wanted to avoid the subject of what had happened between them. Or had nearly happened. Gently placing the towel on the countertop, she turned around to face him. "Don't worry about it. I shouldn't have been snooping."

"That's not what I—" He stopped and pressed his lips together in a thin line. "The book shouldn't have been out. I'd have done the same thing."

Before he looked away, she noticed the pain in his eyes. Yes, Lucas had his own secrets. Without thinking, she took a step toward him. "I'm sorry."

Lucas started to answer, but Harley walked into the kitchen. "Little guy is dead to the world," he said with a chuckle. "If you don't need me for anything else, Lucas, I'll be headed on home."

When Harley had gone, Lucas stood by the table. His gaze went everywhere, except to Rachel, until it landed on the list she'd been working on. He picked it up and looked at it. "This yours?"

"Yes." She slipped it from his fingers, folded it,

and stuffed it in her pocket. With a quick glance at him, she lowered herself to a chair and clasped her hands in front of her on the table. "I want to thank you for letting Cody and me stay."

"I'm the one who should be thanking you," Lucas interrupted. "Can't remember when we've had such good food."

"It's the least I could do." She tried for a smile, but gained nothing from Lucas. "But we can't stay. I was hoping maybe I could get a job at The Rusty Dog. If you'd just tell me where to find this Lou—"

"You don't want to do that," he said, before she could finish. "Jen and Pete will be back soon."

She clenched her hands tighter and focused on them, determined to continue. "The thing is," she began, hesitant to say more than she had to, "I may be at Jenny's longer than a short visit. I can't expect to stay with her without helping out financially. And I don't...I don't really have much money right now."

"Who are you running from?"

Jerking up her head, she stared at him. "Who says I'm running from someone?"

He pinned her with his deep brown eyes. "Pretty obvious, with all those boxes in your trunk."

"I explained about those."

"If there's some problem—"

"No." She tried to smile, but failed. "I can't tell you. I swear it isn't something illegal. It's just...I don't want to involve you."

A muscle in his jaw jumped as he continued to watch her. "I can take care of myself."

She squared her shoulders and shook her head. "I'm sorry. I can't explain. The less you know, the better."

"For who?"

Just the sound of his deep baritone shook her to her core. Before she could answer, she steadied herself. "For you. And for Cody and me, too. We'll be gone before they— Before anyone comes looking for us. As it is, you know we'll be at Jenny's, and that's enough." She stood and paced across the kitchen. "If I can get a job in Deerfork—" She stopped and faced him. "Any job. I just need the means to support myself and Cody."

"You'll be easier to find, if you're working in town."

Rachel shrugged. "Maybe."

His dark gaze held her. "You'll be safer here."

"But you don't know anything about me."

"You rob a bank?"

Rachel's smile was weak. "No."

"Kill somebody?"

Nerves caused her to nearly laugh. "No."

"Then I don't have a problem."

Staying at the Blue Sage was the last thing Rachel wanted to do, but she had to admit, Lucas was right. In town, she'd be more visible. If she could avoid working in public, until Jenny and her husband returned, she'd be safer. And so would Cody. Phyllis and Edward Harris wanted to take her son from her. She wouldn't let that happen. Even if it meant living under the same roof with a man who unsettled her and made her want things she'd given up long ago.

"All right," she agreed. "We'll stay until Jenny gets home."

Lucas was crossing the still-snow-covered yard between the barn and the house when he heard a vehicle coming up the road. In the two days since Rachel had agreed to continue to stay at the ranch, the snow and wind had stopped. He'd canceled the tow truck. He could fix her tire when the time came for her to leave. He had the tools to do it. He and Harley, with the help of Marty and John, had cleared the long drive leading to the road. County crews had cleared the rest. Now, with the temperature rising and the sun out, the snow would be a thing of the past in no time.

He waited at the fence in front of the house for the sheriff's car to come to a stop. Ben Tatum had been a friend since they were kids. It wasn't unusual for the big man to stop in for a visit. But Lucas sensed it wasn't their friendship that now brought the sheriff to his ranch.

"Afternoon, Lucas," Ben said, pulling his bulk from the car. He took his hat from the seat and placed it on his head before closing the door and walking over to where Lucas stood.

Lucas inclined his head. "Ben."

The sheriff tipped back his hat. "That woman still here?"

Lucas eyed him, trying to figure out if Ben was going to add to the problem. Rachel's presence made him uneasy, but it wasn't because he thought she would bring trouble to the ranch. He could handle just about anything. The problem was having her near, living in the same house with her. Smelling her scent in every room. Wanting to reach out and touch her silky cheek, again. And knowing he couldn't. She wasn't a problem. She was a danger.

"Yep, she's here."

Ben looked down as if checking out the shine of his boots. "Mind if I talk to her?"

"What if I do?"

Ben kept his head lowered, but Lucas could feel the man's stare from under the brim of his hat. "Well, I guess I'd have to get a warrant and take her in for questioning."

The mention of something so legal caused Lucas to stiffen. "She done something wrong?"

Letting out a long sigh, Ben lifted his foot onto the fence railing. "I shouldn't be telling you anything, but since this is your ranch…no, far as I know, she hasn't done anything to break the law."

Lucas relaxed and started for the house. "Better come on in, then."

On the porch, they stomped the snow from their boots before Lucas opened the door and ushered the lawman inside. Hell, he didn't know what he could say or not say without getting Rachel in trouble. More trouble than she was obviously already in, anyway. He was relieved to see her standing at the sink, but when she turned as they walked into the kitchen, he saw her face pale.

"You remember Ben," he said, pulling off his hat and indicating the sheriff with a nod.

Her smile was forced. "Yes. This isn't about my license tag, is it, Sheriff? I can assure you that I'll have it and my tire taken care of, before I leave."

Ben stood with his hat in hand. He looked around the room, as if not knowing quite what to do, then pulled out a chair from the table. "No, ma'am. It's not about the plates. Maybe you'd like to sit down?"

With a glance at Lucas, Rachel took the few steps to the chair and lowered herself onto it. Lucas noticed her fingers gripping the edge of the seat and hoped Ben wouldn't see them. Her face was calm, her body language at ease. All except for those white knuckles.

Ben took the seat across the table from her. "Being the sheriff in these parts," he began, then cleared his throat, "it's my job to be curious about strangers. Folks hereabouts have been around for a while. A stranger gets people asking questions."

Rachel nodded. "I can understand that."

Ben hesitated before continuing. "I've known Lucas since we were boys. I'd trust him with my life. If he's letting you stay here at the Blue Sage, then I'd say he trusts you."

Rachel glanced at Lucas with a soft, grateful smile, and he felt a twist in his gut. At that moment, he knew he didn't want her giving Ben any information. He wanted it for himself. He wanted her trust. Enough to tell him what was going on, what had her running. Or who.

"But it's my job to check you out," Ben continued.

The statement sent a chill through Lucas. Would Rachel crack under Ben's questioning?

She didn't bat an eye. "Of course. What do you want to know?"

Ben laid his hat on the table. "Let's start with your name."

"It's Rachel. Rachel Stevens." Her gaze didn't waver from his.

"You're here by yourself?"

"No, my son is with me."

Lucas detected a slight quaver in her voice, but Ben only nodded. "You said you'd taken a wrong turn. Where were you headed?"

"I have friends in the area."

Ben looked up at Lucas with a raised eyebrow.

Until he learned more, Lucas didn't want to mention the Richmonds by name. "They're gone from home for a spell. Rachel and her boy are staying here until they return.''

"And that will be…"

"I'm not sure," Rachel answered. "A few days, I hope."

Lucas stepped forward. "I left a message on their answering machine so they'd know she was looking for them and where to reach her. Until then, she can stay here. Makes more sense than having her travel back to Great Falls. We just got the lane cleared."

Rachel looked up at him, her eyes wide.

"Anything else you need to know, Ben?" His gaze didn't waver from hers. He heard Ben's chair scrape on the floor.

"Nope, I'd say that's about it."

Lucas forced himself to look away from the blue eyes that held him prisoner. "Then I'll walk you back out to your car."

"Sorry to bother you, Ms. Stevens," Ben said as they moved to the door.

"No problem, Sheriff," she answered in a weak voice.

After giving her a brief nod, Lucas stepped out onto the porch and turned to Ben. "What's with the questions?"

Ben looked over his shoulder, as if someone might be watching. "I've had some inquiries about a woman with her description."

A knot formed in Lucas's stomach. "What kind of inquiries?"

"Somebody just looking for a woman and small boy."

Lucas steeled himself against bad news. He needed to know who had Rachel on the run. "What for?"

"Can't be sure," Ben answered. "It's a private investigation."

"Who?"

"Now, Lucas, you know I can't give you that information." Ben buttoned his coat up to his chin. He tipped his hat back and looked at Lucas. "Is Rachel Stevens her name?"

"That's the name she gave me."

Pulling the brim of his hat back down, Ben stepped off the porch and headed for his car. "You know anything she didn't tell me?"

"Nothing important." Lucas followed him and didn't say anything else until they reached the cruiser and the sheriff settled inside. "We've been friends for a long time, Ben."

He placed his hat on the seat next to him and turned to look at Lucas. "You gonna ask me for a favor?"

Lucas nodded and tried to form a request that would net him the best results. "Hold off giving out any information until I can talk to her."

"You think there's something strange going on." It was more a statement than a question.

Lucas let a smile reach his mouth. "Can't say. Maybe there is, maybe there isn't."

"You always were a close one," Ben said with a shake of his head. "Okay. I'll give you a few days. But no longer. Then I'll have to pass on what I've learned."

Lucas stepped away from the car. "Thanks, Ben. I owe you."

Ben leaned his head back and laughed. "You and Harley have been owing me since before I got on the department. But I figure we'll even it out someday."

He looked at Lucas, his eyes narrowed. "Might be sooner than I expected."

Lucas knew an oath when he heard it. Ben would back off for a few days, but if he couldn't get Ben the information he wanted, the sheriff would be back for it himself. That left it up to Lucas. And he wasn't looking forward to interrogating Rachel again.

Rachel didn't know what worried her most, wondering what Lucas might be telling the sheriff, or what the sheriff might be telling Lucas. Had Phyllis and Edward found her? No, if they had, they'd have come to the ranch themselves. But someone was asking questions. If only her license tag hadn't come loose, the sheriff might never have noticed her. But if she had stopped on the road when she'd first noticed his lights, he would have had a make on her. She knew she should count herself lucky that she'd turned down the road to the Blue Sage. She just wasn't sure if that luck was good or bad.

It still surprised her that Lucas had helped her avoid questions without giving away too much. She had told him all she could. She couldn't answer any more questions. The less she said, the better. The less they were around each other, the better.

When she heard the heavy footsteps of boots on the porch, she slipped from the kitchen and up the stairs to check on Cody. She didn't want to face Lucas. She knew she should thank him, but she was afraid it would only give him the chance to question her. And she would be forced to answer him. He had come to her rescue. She owed him that much. But she wanted to put it off for as long as possible.

Cody slept peacefully under the quilt on the bed

they shared. She sat on the edge and finger-combed the hair from his forehead. Her baby. The baby Steven hadn't wanted because it would tie them down. But she'd wanted to be tied down. She had wanted a family like the one she'd lost when she was no bigger than Cody. If it hadn't been for her son—

"We need to talk."

Rachel jumped at the sound of Lucas's voice.

He was propped in the doorway, watching her. His gaze moved over her like a lover's hands, touching each inch of her and making her heart thud.

Shoving away from the door frame, he hesitated. "I'll be in the office."

She bit down on a lip that threatened to tremble and nodded. The time had come to tell Lucas the truth. She couldn't avoid it any longer. She only hoped she could trust him with it.

After making certain Cody was still asleep, she headed downstairs on weak knees. At the door to the ranch office, she stopped and took a deep breath. "You wanted to talk to me, Lucas?"

He looked up from the papers on his desk. "Come in," he said, shoving the papers aside, and stood. "And close the door."

A shiver of fear—or was it anticipation?—swept through her as she stepped into the room and closed the door behind her. She stood, uncertain whether she should pour it all out to him or let him take the lead. She decided on the latter.

"Sit down, Rachel. I won't bite."

With a stiff nod, she swallowed the lump in her throat and took the chair where she'd sat with the photo album. She didn't have the nerve to look around to see if it was still nearby.

He moved to sit on the corner of the desk and waited. Under his gaze, she felt the heat of a blush on her cheeks and kept her head lowered.

When he spoke, his voice was soft but firm. "You're going to have to tell me everything this time, Rachel."

The thought petrified her. Her mouth went dry, and she could feel her palms dampening. "Did...did the sheriff get the information he wanted?"

"Enough to keep him satisfied for a few days."

She could only nod. She couldn't even lift her head to look at him. Somehow, she had to find the courage she knew was buried under the avalanche of feelings this man caused.

"You've danced around the truth long enough. I want to know what's going on." His voice was slow and lazy, but strength and determination lurked beneath the surface.

"I—I—" Rachel shook her head, unable to tell him what she knew she must. She didn't hear him move, didn't know what was happening, until she felt his hands on her arms, lifting her to her feet.

"Dammit, Rachel," his gruff voice raked at her conscience, "I came as close to lying for you than I ever have for anybody. You owe me an explanation."

Jerking away, she moved to stand at the window. The sun reflected off the white snow, blinding her, but she didn't turn around. Her heart pounded in her ears. Her skin burned beneath her shirt where he'd touched her. Why did this man cause these reactions in her?

She took a deep, steadying breath and turned to look at him. "Yes, and I do thank you, Lucas," she finally managed. "But I didn't ask you to lie, and you didn't. The only lie was mine. My name."

"I figured that. I went along with it." He rubbed at the back of his neck and lowered his head, shaking it. "I don't know why, though," he muttered. When he looked at her again, his eyes held accusation and burned into her soul. "Someone is looking for you. You know who it is."

She wanted to look anywhere else but at him. She couldn't. He held her gaze like a magnet to steel. Her words stuck in her throat, but she forced them out. "Yes, my husband's parents."

"Your husband is deceased."

Nodding, she was able to look away. "Steven died two years ago. Six months later, his parents came to me and offered to take Cody off my hands." She glared at Lucas. "Off my hands! I couldn't believe it. I told them I was his mother, and I would continue to raise him."

"But they didn't agree."

"At the time, they let it drop." She lowered herself to the windowsill, unable to tell him the whole story, how they'd had her followed, until they could find something to use against her. And they had. "They don't believe a woman can raise a child alone," she said, instead. "I don't have much money, Lucas. They have more than they need."

His lips thinned. "Your husband didn't leave you anything? Insurance?"

She shook her head, remembering how Steven had cashed in his insurance policy to pay off his gambling debts. That had only been the beginning.

"You've worked, haven't you?"

"At any job I could find. I don't have the training for anything that pays well." She thought of the job that had been her downfall. She wasn't ashamed she had taken it or of what she'd done, but she couldn't bring herself to tell him about it. It was easier to let him think it was about money, not that they wanted Cody to replace his father.

"Nothing will be good enough for them. I could never raise Cody in the wealthy environment they can offer," she told him.

"You've been running for a year and a half?"

Tears stung her eyes. "Most of it. Cody and I have always lived in big cities. I'd hoped it would work as a camouflage, make it more difficult for them to find us. But they always do. I thought that by coming here to Jenny's, it would give me time to stop running for a while. As far as I know, they don't know anything about her."

"I didn't tell Ben who your friends are, if that's what you're thinking."

"I didn't think you did. I don't know how to thank you."

"If you'd told me—"

"I couldn't." She stood on wobbly legs, wishing she could tell him everything. "I couldn't have you dragged into this. Phyllis and Edward Harris are determined to take Cody from me. When they find me this time, I expect them to have a court order."

"Then get your own attorney."

"I can't afford an attorney, Lucas. If I could, I would have fought them long ago. But money is power. If you don't know that, I do."

"They may have traced you to the area, that's all. They don't know for sure that you're here."

"But the sheriff will have to tell them, won't he?"

Lucas hesitated before nodding. "Ben will wait a few days, but he'll have to tell them something."

"Then we have to leave. I can't stay and risk them finding us." She crossed the room to the door, wondering where she and Cody would go. Would they be safe in Great Falls? Or would they have to go farther? To another state? And where would she get the money? Unshed tears choked her as she reached for the doorknob.

Lucas's hand on hers stopped her. "You're safer here."

She looked up into eyes as dark as the night sky. "For how long?"

A parade of emotions crossed his face. "If I tell Ben—"

Rachel grabbed his arm with her free hand. "No, you can't tell him anything. He'll have to tell them I'm here."

"Maybe not. Ben's a good guy." He pulled her hand from the doorknob but didn't release her. "Let's see what happens. I'll sound him out without telling him anything. Pete and Jen will be home soon."

She dropped her hand from his arm and stepped back. "I can't let you take the risk of having us here. I don't know what Phyllis and Edward might do."

"They can't do anything, if they don't know you're here," he pointed out, releasing her.

Rachel considered his words. If they could only keep her in-laws at bay until Jenny returned... But to do that, she'd have to ask Lucas to lie for her. Possibly even Harley and the hands. She was thankful that Lucas had kept her from seeking work. It would have dragged more people into her web of deceit. She'd never asked anyone to lie for her before. She didn't know if she could start now.

"I can't ask you to do this, Lucas." She opened the door, ready to step out of the room, until he spoke.

"Rachel, I'm offering." His mouth slanted in a smile. "I'll find a way to hold Ben off, for a while. When Pete and Jen get back, you can go there. Nobody will be any wiser."

Other than packing up and leaving with no money and nowhere to go, Rachel realized she didn't have a choice. "All right," she conceded. "But if you hear from the sheriff that someone is coming, promise me that you'll tell me. Cody and I will leave. You'll never know where we're going, so you won't have to lie."

Lucas didn't answer.

"Promise me, Lucas."

After several moments, he inclined his head. "I'll see what I can find out from Ben. Until then, you stay put."

Rachel nodded.

On her way upstairs to check on Cody, she wondered if she'd done the right thing. Nothing had gone right since she had arrived at the Blue Sage. She should have known she couldn't keep the truth from a man like Lucas, but she'd told him all she could. He couldn't help her without eventually bringing trouble to himself. She wouldn't let that happen. If she had any indication that Cody's grandparents were getting close, she would leave.

Chapter Five

Lucas stood in the doorway, staring after Rachel. Running a hand through his hair, he took an uncertain step back. What had he done? He had wanted her to leave. Having her in the house, so near, yet forbidden, was more than he could stand. But he wanted her. The more time he spent with her, the more his need to touch her, to hold her, grew. It was wrong. He shouldn't be feeling that way about her. About any woman. Hadn't he learned his lesson?

But Rachel wasn't anything like Debra. Rachel's goodness shone brightly in her blue eyes, in the way she cared for her son. Her strength was evident in the way she protected him, and her love for him was a thing of beauty. He could think of only one woman who had been a better mother.

An image of the woman who'd given birth to him and raised him until she lost her battle with cancer made him catch his breath. His heart ached. She hadn't had an easy life, but she had done everything in her power to make his the best she could. Too bad he was more like his father than he was like her.

He crossed the room and sank onto the chair behind his desk. Pressing his face into his hands, he took a deep breath and let it out.

Rachel reminded him of his mother.

He sat there, for some time, remembering how his mother had sacrificed for him, then how she had valiantly battled the disease that had taken her from him. And he tried to put Rachel out of his mind. When the phone rang, it jarred him back to the present.

"It's just me," Harley greeted him.

"I was just thinking of my mother."

"Yep, she was a saint. My daddy always said so," Harley said in a voice deep with reverence. "Rachel does remind me of her." He paused for a moment. "She stayin'?"

"For a while." Lucas briefly gave Harley the information Rachel had shared. "She has some crazy idea she's going to bring trouble," he added when he'd finished.

Harley snorted. "Not likely. I told John and Marty to keep it to themselves that she's stayin' here."

Lucas cradled the phone to his ear with his shoulder and picked up a pen, rolling it between his palms. He knew his hired hands would keep quiet. Both men had fallen head over heels for their visitor. If they knew there was some kind of trouble, they'd be more than willing to help.

"So she told you everything?"

"Most of it, I'd say."

"How'd you get it out of her?" Harley's voice had dropped to a near whisper.

"I just did." Lucas tossed the pen to the desk, disgusted with himself for the way he had treated her. And for the feelings she aroused in him. He didn't want to care. But he did. Too much.

Harley was quiet for a moment, then cleared his throat. "Terri and I were talkin'..."

Alerted by the tone in Harley's voice, Lucas jerked to attention. "What?"

"Well, you see, I bet Rachel hasn't been out and had a good time for so long, she doesn't remember what it's like."

"So?" Lucas didn't want to hear what his stepbrother might be thinking. But it wouldn't do any good to stop him. The more Lucas might protest, the harder Harley would push.

"Well, Terri and I are plannin' to go to The Rusty Dog tonight. See, I had to tell her what's goin' on. She feels real sorry for Rachel."

"Terri doesn't even know the half of it yet."

"She will. I'll fill her in tonight. But I was thinkin' maybe you and Rachel might like to come along."

Lucas could only imagine what spending the evening with Harley and the two women would be like. He didn't want anything to do with it. The less time he spent in Rachel's company, the better. She and Cody would be leaving soon, moving right out of his life. And wasn't that what he wanted? No matter how much he might think he wanted her, getting to know her any better than he already did would be dangerous. He'd thought he didn't have a heart after Debra, but Rachel and her troubles had caused an ache he had no other explanation for. He didn't want it to become anything more. He knew what caring for a woman brought with it.

He pushed away from the desk and stood, intending

to put an end to Harley's scheme. "You three have a good time. I'll stay and keep an eye on Cody."

"Marty told the little guy he'd teach him to play checkers tonight," Harley said, before Lucas even had a chance to take a breath. "We won't be out late. Rachel won't mind."

Lucas searched his mind for another excuse. "She might. She doesn't know Marty."

"She won't be leavin' the boy with him for more than a couple of hours," Harley coaxed. "And you need to get out, too, Lucas."

Lucas closed his eyes and counted to five. The only time he stopped at The Rusty Dog was to grab a few beers. Sometimes he'd bring home a bucket of ribs, but he avoided the place like he would a horse that had been grazing in locoweed. He kept to the ranch as much as possible. Tongues tended to wag, and he figured they were still wagging from when he'd been married to Debra. She had hated the place, and everyone knew it.

"Rachel might not like The Rusty Dog," he pointed out.

"She's not highfalutin, Lucas. Not like—" He sighed. "Not like some. If you don't go, Rachel might think it's somethin' personal."

Lucas wanted to tell him it was something personal, but he kept quiet. "We'll leave it up to her," he said instead and wished he'd bitten his tongue off for saying that much.

"She might need a little encouragement," Harley suggested.

"That's your job," Lucas growled into the phone. He wasn't going to get railroaded into this scheme, and that was that.

* * *

Harley did his job well, much to Lucas's disgust. Seated shoulder to shoulder and thigh to thigh in one of the more secluded half-circle booths in The Rusty Dog, he had to remind himself that the heat he felt was because of the full occupancy of the room. Not because of the proximity of Rachel's soft curves and the scent of peaches teasing him.

"I've never been back East," Terri said, after they placed their order for a double family bucket of ribs.

Lucas hadn't failed to notice how well the two women had taken to one another. A stranger would have thought they'd been friends all their lives. But that's the way Terri was and he suspected Rachel was, too.

"It's…different," Rachel answered. "The wide-open spaces here leave me breathless. In the East, you can't go more than a few miles before running into civilization of some kind."

With every word she spoke, her body moved next to his. Lucas felt her breath moving in and out, and gritted his teeth against the reaction it was causing in him.

"No, that's not Montana," Terri agreed. "Do you like it? I mean the isolation around here."

Rachel nodded. "It's like a breath of fresh air. With the snow, I haven't had much of a chance to get out and enjoy it, but driving through, I got a sense of…oh, I don't know. Peace, I guess."

Lucas wished she would give him some wide-open space and some peace. He was getting more uncomfortable by the minute. He was already on the edge of the vinyl seat. If he moved any farther to his left, he would be on the floor. A glance at Harley proved there was room on the other end for everyone to move down that way. Lucas tried to catch his eye, but Harley was intent on the conversation between Terri and Rachel. Telling him to give them more room would be rude, so Lucas kept quiet. Perspiration popped out on his forehead.

"—didn't you, Lucas?"

He jerked around to look at Terri. "What?"

"Harley said when you were kids, you went to the East Coast, but you didn't like it."

Lucas moved another inch to his left and planted his feet firmly on the floor. The action jammed his thigh against Rachel's and only served to remind him that she had worn a dress for the occasion instead of the jeans she'd been living in. That meant less fabric between them, he thought. His mouth went dry. What had Terri said to him?

Rachel's wistful voice brought him out of it. "I was born near Virginia Beach, but grew up farther north in Maryland. I remember spending a lot of time on the beach with my mother when I was very young."

"A Southern belle," Terri said with a smile.

"Not really," Rachel said. Lucas felt her stiffen beside him before she continued. "My parents died when I was seven. After that, I lived in foster homes. Nine of them by the time I made it through high school."

Terri placed her hand on Rachel's. "I'm so sorry. What an awful way to grow up."

"That explains it." Lucas didn't know he'd spoken, until the words were out of his mouth. But it did explain her driving need to keep her son with her, at all costs.

His chest constricted when Rachel looked up at him, a soft smile on her lips. "It wasn't that bad," she said before turning to the others. "I lived with some wonderful families. They weren't all good, but most of them were. And the ones that weren't, I didn't stay in long."

Terri propped her chin in her hand. "I grew up with three older brothers. Most times it was pure hell. They're still overprotective."

Harley tipped his head back and laughed. "That's an understatement. Not only did her daddy give me the third degree the first time I picked her up for a date, but her brothers each gave me some advice before we ever made it out to the car. Only the advice was more threat than anything. I'd have been the same way if I'd had a baby sister, though," he added, giving Terri a hug. "Can't blame 'em one bit."

"Poor thing," Terri said, patting his chest. "All you had was a stepbrother."

"But I was a good one," Lucas interjected, standing up for himself. "Taught him how to fight."

"Only because we never could get along," Harley said with a laugh. "When Lucas was twelve, his daddy left to travel the rodeo circuit and didn't come back. His mama finally filed for divorce after two years. She married my daddy when we were fifteen."

"Took us a year to be able to look at each other without throwing a punch," Lucas added with a chuckle. He remembered how jealous he'd been of the attention his mother had given the interloper.

"What happened?" Rachel asked.

Lucas shrugged, and the movement brushed his arm against Rachel's, sending another heat wave through his body. "We just found some common ground."

Harley's shoulders shook with laughter. "If it hadn't been for Jimmy Lee Hawthorne, we might never have gotten along. Jimmy Lee made some comments about my daddy and Lucas's mama.'' Harley's grin widened. ''But he didn't mention either one of them again. At least not around us.''

The memory of the schoolyard fight was still strong in Lucas's mind. It had brought him and Harley together, and after that, there'd never been anyone who could separate the two of them. Not even Debra, although she'd tried.

Harley kept the evening lively with stories of their teenage years. Terri and Rachel added a few of their own. But Lucas didn't say much. He was too busy hanging on to Rachel's every word and wondering how he was going to deal with his rampaging hormones until Jen and Pete returned.

The weather turned warm and the snow melted within days. Rachel was eager to get away from the Blue Sage Ranch. Being around Lucas Callahan had her on edge. She tried her best to ignore how her body seemed to melt whenever he was in the room, but each time she saw him, it became more impossible. He'd spoken only a few words to her since their evening out, and she was relieved. But every now and then, she would catch him watching her. He always managed to look away too quickly for her to read anything in his eyes, but each time she felt herself drawn to him even more.

Marty and John joined them for the noon meal each day, and she did her best to avoid talking to the men. She liked the two neighboring cowboys, but the looks Lucas shot them whenever they spoke to her caused her to keep her conversation to a minimum.

Rachel watched Cody, noticing his reserve with the men had disappeared. He could barely sit still at the table while the men finished their meal. "Lucas said I could help him in the barn," he announced, bouncing in his chair.

The mention of Lucas's name caused her to look at the man, but he didn't bother to glance at either her son or her. "It's up to Lucas," she told Cody.

Lucas answered with a shrug before pushing away from the table and standing. "Bring him out when you all finish up here."

Hoping no one noticed, Rachel watched him stride with purpose to the door, his mouth set in a firm, straight line. She had rarely seen him smile since they'd arrived at the ranch, but he'd been almost pleasant during their dinner at The Rusty Dog. Pleasant, at least, for Lucas. She had seen him smile that night and had even heard him laugh, something she'd never expected. It had been a lovely dinner, but she'd been eager to get it over with. Sitting next to him had been more torture than she had been prepared for. But since then, he had been more silent than usual. Was he sorry he'd exposed so much of himself?

While Lucas pulled on his coat, the other men and Cody got to their feet. Marty and John didn't waste any time getting out the door behind Lucas. Harley helped Cody with his coat, the boy asking questions with every button through the hole.

"Are you sure he won't be any trouble?" she asked, before the two stepped out of the house.

"If he is, I'll be surprised," Harley answered.

Rachel chewed her bottom lip. "But Lucas—"

"Don't pay any attention to Lucas. He's in one of his moods. Don't know what's botherin' him, but maybe havin' Cody help him will change things." He whispered to Cody, and the boy ducked under his arm,

racing down the porch steps. "Come on out and check
on him later, if you think I'm wrong."

Uncertain, she nodded. When Harley had gone, she
busied herself with clearing the table and cleaning up
after the meal preparation. She had managed to feel at
home in the ranch's kitchen, and she had the chore
done in no time. Not knowing what else to do with
herself, and knowing she would only be in the way if
she were to check on her son so soon, she searched
for something to do. She rummaged through the cabinets and found the ingredients for a cake. Pulling out
bowls and measuring cups, she felt a sense of peace.
Baking reminded her of her mother. Along with the
memories of walking the beach, it was one of the few
she had.

Rachel allowed herself to look out the window. She
hadn't wanted to check on Cody for fear Lucas would
think she didn't trust him with her son. It wasn't that
she didn't trust the man. She was afraid the exuber-
ance Cody had begun to show at the ranch activities
would irritate Lucas. She didn't think she could handle
those brooding frowns much longer, and she longed
to see even a hint of a smile from him.

Pushing aside the curtain at the door, she looked
across the yard to the barn. Her fingers closed around
the fabric and her breath caught in her throat. Outside
in the corral, Cody sat astride a horse. He looked so
small and vulnerable atop the huge animal. If he were
to fall... Fear gripped her heart and she forced herself
to move.

She jerked the door open and stumbled onto the
porch. "Cody," she called to him in a wobbling voice.

Her son turned his head to look at her, putting him
off balance. He tipped to the side, but Lucas, who

stood at the horse's head, was quick to put a hand out to stop Cody from toppling to the ground.

She wasn't sure how she got there, but she reached the corral fence with knees weak from fear. "Cody, get down, right now."

"Aw, Mom."

Lucas spoke to him in a low voice that she couldn't hear and then turned to look at her. "He's okay. You surprised him. I won't let anything happen to him."

Crossing her arms on her chest, she glared at him. "Get down, Cody," she repeated without looking at her son. "You'll get hurt."

Cody didn't move. "It was my fault, Mom. I wasn't paying attention. Lucas told me not to let anything dis...dis..."

"Distract him," Lucas stated. He turned to Cody. "Hold on to that saddle horn." Watching until the boy obeyed, he turned to Rachel. "If you don't want him on the horse—"

"I thought he was helping you in the barn," she said, her heart still pounding.

"I thought Cody might like to use the saddle he cleaned up." He didn't make a move to remove the boy from the horse. "If he's going to live around here, he needs to learn to ride. Most kids know how to ride not long after they learn to walk. Cody's already behind."

She dropped her arms, clenching her hands into fists to keep them from trembling, and climbed through the fence. "He's never been around animals. Anything could happen to him. He might get scared, he might—"

Lucas's eyes narrowed when he looked at her. "He's safe with me."

"He's not safe with anybody! He could fall. The horse could throw him or run off with him."

The frown on his face deepened. "Stop babying the boy, Rachel." His voice was low, almost a threat.

She couldn't believe her ears. What did this man know about children? What did he know about Cody? "Don't you dare tell me how to raise my son."

Something flared in his eyes before he reached up and took Cody off the horse, setting him safely on the ground. Her son's bottom lip trembled, and his eyes glistened with tears. He wouldn't look at her.

"He's as safe up there as if I were riding with him," Lucas said in a soft but menacing voice.

"You don't have a clue," she snapped, snatching Cody into her arms.

Cody pulled away from her and scowled. "I'm not going to get hurt, Mom."

"You don't know that," she told him, reaching for him.

He backed away from her. "Lucas could already ride by himself before he started school."

It was the belligerence in his eyes that set her off. Cody rarely argued or even disagreed with her. "You aren't Lucas. It was different for him. Now, go on into the house and clean up."

She noticed the quiver in his chin when he turned to obey, but his shoulders remained squared and his back stiff. Something about the way he carried himself reminded her of Lucas, and that made her even angrier.

When she turned back, Lucas was leading the horse to the barn, his stride long and powerful. Like an animal, she thought. An animal who knew nothing about raising young.

Her anger flared even more. Lucas needed to be put in his place and understand he wasn't to make decisions concerning her son. And she was going to tell him.

As he entered the barn, Lucas regretted telling Rachel to stop babying Cody. What did he know about raising a kid? His own child had died before ever drawing his first breath. Lucas had never known what it was to be responsible for a young life. Debra had stolen that from him. His own father hadn't been around enough to set an example, and by the time his mother had married Charlie Peterson, Lucas had been past the age of learning much about fatherhood.

He wished he could take back his words. Not only had he made her mad, he'd hurt her. And that was something he didn't want to do. It all proved what a bad father he would have made if his child had lived. Maybe Debra had done him a favor, after all.

"Mr. Callahan."

He looked up from the saddle he was repairing to see Rachel storm through the barn door. He placed the length of leather stripping aside and straightened. "Look, I'm—"

"You look," she said, her blue eyes blazing. "You never should have put Cody on that horse."

Stepping around the saddle, he took three steps toward her and stopped. "I thought—"

"No, you didn't think. You didn't think at all."

"I know. I'm—"

She planted her fists on her hips. "You don't know a thing about raising kids. Did you give a thought to what might happen if Cody fell? He could have broken something. His arms, his legs, his *neck*. You're irre-

sponsible. You're—'' Her face went bright red and she
slammed her mouth shut. She closed her eyes and took
a deep breath.

Lucas couldn't remember ever feeling so small. Rachel had pegged him. He hadn't thought. Not about
Cody, or about what could happen. All he knew was
that by Cody's age, he'd been riding the ranch with
his dad. When his dad was home, which wasn't often.
But he'd grown up on the ranch. He'd been on a horse
since he was a baby. It was second nature to him. But
it wasn't for Cody.

She couldn't have been more right about him. He'd
have made a lousy father. He *didn't* have a clue.

"I'm sorry, Lucas," she said on a sigh.

The look in her eyes when she opened them nearly
buckled his knees. "You don't owe me an apology. I
owe you one. You're right. I don't know anything
about kids."

She shook her head and avoided looking at him.
"No, I'm too overprotective. You were right. It was
unfair of me to say that to you. You don't know about
being a father because you've never been one."

He opened his mouth to tell her he almost had been,
but he closed it. He hadn't even told Harley how he'd
felt when Debra lost their baby. He wasn't about to
tell this woman, who would be leaving in a few days.
A woman he didn't want to see leave. A woman he
had been trying not to fantasize about. And failing,
repeatedly.

She looked up at him, nearly bringing him to his
knees with the tears he saw filling her eyes. "He's my
baby, Lucas. He's all I have. If anything happened to
him…"

Lucas forced himself not to move. He had never

seen Rachel's vulnerability. Since the moment she'd sped into the ranch yard, he'd seen many sides of her. Strength, determination, fear, kindness, laughter. The list went on and on. But he'd never thought she might be vulnerable. He wanted to take her in his arms and hold her. Let her know he was there for her. But if he held her, he wouldn't be able to stop there. He'd been dreaming of kissing her for days. Finding out if her lips tasted as sweet as she smelled. Just thinking of it brought his body to life.

Rachel's soft voice forced him out of his dream and back to reality. "Will you forgive me, Lucas? You've been so kind to me. I don't know what I would have done without you."

Her unselfish plea was more than he could take. Four long steps brought him within touching distance of her. He fisted his hands to keep from reaching for her, but when she looked up at him, her eyes shimmering, he couldn't stop himself. With a groan, he reached for her, dragging her to him. His gaze locked with her surprised one as he lowered his head. He didn't hesitate. He couldn't. He brought his mouth down to hers, crushing her lips beneath his.

She stiffened in his arms, her palms planted on his chest. He expected her to push him away, but instead, he felt her relax. Her arms slid up to encircle his neck, and she pressed against him. He moved his hands from her shoulders to her back, holding her to him while he touched his tongue to her lips. Her answering gasp opened her mouth to him and he plunged to search the depths. The scent of peaches invaded him, the taste of sweetness consumed him. He slid his hands lower, cupping her bottom to lift her up and against the ache she caused. Her fingers tangled in his hair, while a voice deep in his head told him he had made a fatal mistake, but he couldn't stop.

She must have heard the same voice, because she tore her mouth from his. Her ragged breath whispered from her parted lips, drawing his gaze to their kiss-swollen plumpness. He wanted more. So much more.

He dropped his hands when he looked into her eyes. Fear, unadulterated and clear, shone in them. Before he had a chance to form a thought, she turned and ran for the door, disappearing into the sunlight outside.

The impact of what he had done hit him full force. With a groan, he collapsed against the nearest post.

She'd never forgive him. Hell, he'd never forgive himself.

Chapter Six

Rachel wasn't certain how she made it back to the house. If it had only been her cheeks burning, she wouldn't have cared. But the kiss she'd shared with Lucas had set every molecule of her body on fire. And yes, she had shared in it. In fact, she'd wanted it, desperately.

"Mom?"

She closed the door behind her and slipped out of her coat. While she hung it on the peg in the kitchen, she attempted to pull herself together before she faced her son.

"What is it, Cody?" She turned, her thoughts stampeding through her mind like a herd of wild horses, stirring up the dust of old emotions.

He stood with his chin touching his chest. "I'm all cleaned up now."

His defeated stance brought her to her knees in front of him. "Oh, Cody, I'm so sorry," she said, scooping him into her arms. Her eyes stung with tears, but she held them back. "I wasn't being fair to you. I was afraid you'd be hurt. That horse is so big and—"

"I'm six years old, Mom," came his muffled reply.

She smiled and held him away so she could see him. "Yes, you're growing up. You're not my baby anymore. I need to remember that." Finger-combing his hair, she took a deep breath. "Do you want to go back out and try again?"

He looked toward the door and shook his head.

"I promise I won't interfere, sweetie."

"Don't you trust Lucas?"

She nodded, unable for the moment to speak. She did trust Lucas with Cody. But with herself? Maybe it was herself she didn't trust. In fact, as far as Cody was concerned, Lucas could probably do a better job with him than she'd been doing. Cody would never grow up to be a man if she didn't start letting him now. If she didn't watch it, he'd be twenty and still a mama's boy, just like— Rachel's mind came to a sudden halt. *Just like Steven.*

The thought shook her, badly. Was she doing the same thing to their son that Steven's parents had done to him? And wasn't that exactly what she was trying to keep from happening? Phyllis and Edward had doted on Steven. In the beginning, she hadn't noticed how much it had affected him. With time, it became more and more apparent. They would never admit he had done anything wrong. She couldn't let that happen to Cody.

For the time being, Lucas was the perfect influence on her son. It was plain to see that Cody worshiped him. What could it hurt?

It could hurt me. But she wouldn't let it. Keeping

Cody was what was important. Not these growing feelings she had for Lucas.

After giving Cody a shaky hug, she got to her feet. "I'll talk to Lucas. If he can take some time tomorrow, maybe he can give you an extralong lesson. How would that be?"

He looked up at her, his eyes sparkling. "That'd be great!"

She hugged him again, then hustled him upstairs to play with the meager assortment of toys they had brought with them. A glance at her watch told her she needed to start the cake she had planned to bake. She'd make it special and decorate it. Maybe she could offer it as a symbol of apology.

She had just closed the oven door on the filled cake pans when she heard the kitchen door open behind her. Afraid it might be Lucas, she stepped to the cabinets and began an aimless search for nothing.

"Rachel?"

Her breath caught, and a hot flush swept through her. She didn't want to face Lucas so soon after their encounter in the barn. Just the thought of how she'd responded to his kiss, how her body had come alive in his arms, left her cheeks burning and her blood pulsing in a sensual rhythm.

"I'm real sorry about Cody," he said from behind her.

She forced herself to turn and look at him. His remorse was obvious. But was it for the horse ride or for the kiss? "No. I'm the one who's sorry. I know you wouldn't let anything happen to him. I overreacted."

He lowered his head, hiding his face. "I'd never let

anything happen to him. I should've asked you if it was okay to put him on that horse.''

She couldn't argue with that. Cody was her son and she was responsible for him. But she needed to prove that she trusted this cowboy. ''From now on, you have my permission to teach Cody to ride.''

He looked up, almost smiling. ''Good. He'll be riding around the ranch in no time. He's a real natural.'' He stood, looking uncomfortable, as if he had something else to say. But he remained silent.

Busying herself in an attempt to act as if nothing had happened between them, she couldn't help smiling to herself. Her son, a natural. If they stayed in the area, maybe Cody could have a horse of his own. But plans for the future were impossible to make. She never knew from one day to the next where she and Cody would be. These last few days at the Blue Sage were the longest they'd stayed in one place for weeks. But if the sheriff was already asking questions, it was a certainty that Phyllis and Edward weren't far behind.

Rachel turned around. ''If someone came looking for us after Jenny gets back, would you tell them where we went?''

''Are you asking if I'd lie for you?''

She studied the solemn look on his face and nodded. ''I guess that's exactly what I'm asking.''

His eyes narrowed. ''I'm not good at lying. But if the truth meant you losing that boy, I think I could do a pretty good impression of it.''

She closed her eyes, sighing with relief. Opening them, she attempted a smile of appreciation. ''I wouldn't ask you to do it, if it weren't necessary.''

He nodded. ''I know that. Maybe it won't be.''

Wishing he was right, she shook her head. ''They'll

find us here. They haven't failed yet. We've only been a step ahead of them for the past two months."

Before she could say more, Cody burst into the kitchen and threw himself at Lucas. "Did Mom ask if I could have another riding lesson tomorrow?"

Lucas lifted him onto the edge of the table. "She gave me permission to teach you any time."

"Can we do it tomorrow?"

Rachel was embarrassed by her son's rude behavior. "Cody, don't pester Lucas."

Cody swiveled around on the table to stare at her with wide, innocent eyes. "I'm not pestering, Mom. I'm asking."

"It's all right," Lucas interrupted, then turned to Cody. "Why don't you go ask Harley if he needs some help."

"Sure." Cody jumped down from the table with Lucas's help. Racing to the door, he grabbed his coat and stuffed his arms in the sleeves.

"Button up," she reminded him, before he scooted out the door. She turned to Lucas, wincing at the sound of the door slamming. "I'm sorry. He's not usually like this. It must be because he's been cooped up for so long. First in tiny apartments, then in the car." She stopped and smiled. "It must be these wide-open spaces."

Lucas took a seat at the table. "You like it here? In Montana?"

She thought about it. It was nothing like she had ever known. "Yes. Yes, I think I could get used to it in no time," she admitted.

"Debra never could," he said in a voice so quiet, Rachel almost missed it.

Seeing the way he ducked his head and clamped his

jaw shut, she knew the comment had slipped out. She had questions, but she didn't know if she could ask them. She doubted he would answer them, but, still, it was worth a try.

She turned to a pot soaking on the stove, and stirred the soapy contents, as if she were cooking something. Her hand shook, and it took a concentrated effort to keep the spoon from banging against the side of the pan as she tried to keep her voice nonchalant. "Debra was your wife?"

He didn't answer for several seconds. "Yes."

Rachel wasn't certain how to continue. His curt answer told her not to pursue the subject. She suspected that something about his former wife or their marriage had made him distant and untrusting. She had thought him coldhearted when she had first met him. Now she knew different. She was slowly learning he wasn't at all what he seemed. If his kiss was any indication of the warmth of his heart—

Rachel put the brakes on the unbidden memory, heat flooding her face, then spreading through her body. But she had to go on. This was her chance to question him. She couldn't let her attraction to him distract her.

"How long were you married?" she asked when she gained control again.

"Almost four years. If I'd been smart—"

When he didn't continue, she glanced over her shoulder to see the frown on his face. She wanted to encourage him. Knowing about him would be helpful.

Admit it, Rache, it isn't because it would be helpful. You want to know everything about him.

"Look, she was no good," he continued with obvious reluctance. "And when she left, she took everything she could."

"She didn't get the Blue Sage."

"She got everything else she could." He lifted his gaze to hers. "And I don't mean money, either."

Rachel didn't realize she had moved to the table where he sat, until she found herself on the chair across from him. "What happened?"

Lucas stared at her, his eyes revealing the pain he still felt. She could feel it, too, and her heart ached for him. She wanted to do something to help. He had done so much for her and Cody. But unless she knew what had caused it—

His chair scraped the floor, when he pushed away from the table. "Nothing you need to be concerned about."

But she was concerned! She could see how badly he was hurting, and it hurt her, too. Whatever had happened, it hadn't been "nothing." But she knew she couldn't push him. She hadn't been completely truthful with him. It wasn't right to ask him to do what she wasn't willing to do herself.

As he left the kitchen, more silent and brooding than usual, she shook her head and sighed. What did it matter? She couldn't allow herself any feelings for anyone, no matter what her body craved. Her only need was to keep Cody with her. She needed to keep that in mind, and nothing else. Especially not a man like Lucas.

Rachel crossed the kitchen, carrying a load of laundry, and glanced at the cake she had decorated the night before. The colored bits of marshmallows she had picked out of a box of cereal looked all right, but she wished she had had something more.

She hadn't seen Lucas since she'd questioned him. It had been late when she'd finally climbed the stairs to bed, and Lucas had still been in the barn. He had never made an appearance. She wondered if he'd waited until most of the lights in the house were out before coming inside, and suspected he was avoiding her as much as she was him.

When the phone rang, she balanced the basket of clothes on one hip and grabbed the receiver without thinking.

"Rachel, is that you?"

Nearly dropping the basket at the sound of the blessedly familiar voice, Rachel propped herself against the wall. Knees weak with relief, it took all her effort to stay upright. "Jenny? Oh, Jenny, thank God."

Her friend's questions ran together. "What are you doing at the Blue Sage? When did you get to Montana? Why didn't you tell me you were coming?"

Rachel couldn't stop the laughter that bubbled inside her. "I know I should have told you we were coming, but I never imagined you'd be gone."

"If only I'd known." Jenny's voice was filled with regret. "This crazy trip was spur-of-the-moment. We suddenly decided we needed to get away."

Rachel felt a ripple of panic. "You aren't home?"

It was Jenny's turn to laugh. "Of course we're home. I just walked in and heard Lucas's message on the answering machine." There was a silent pause on the other end. "Is something wrong, Rache? Cody's okay, isn't he?"

"Cody is fine." She wasn't sure what to tell Jenny.

She hadn't shared her problems concerning Steven's parents. Jenny knew there'd been things happening in the marriage, but Rachel had never elaborated.

She tried to laugh, but it shook with nervousness. "I hope you have an extra bedroom."

"Of course we do," Jenny assured her. "For as long as you can stay. Our house is almost as big as that one." Another short pause followed. "Lucas has behaved himself, hasn't he?"

"He's been a perfect gentlemen." A picture of Lucas's frown passed through her mind, quickly followed by the feel of his lips on hers. Rachel felt her knees turn rubbery again, glad Jenny couldn't see her.

"He hasn't growled too much or bitten your head off?" Jenny asked with a laugh.

"No, he's been...very kind." Rachel wasn't sure those were the right words to describe the man, but she didn't want to go into it. She didn't plan to share anything that had happened between them with anyone. Not even Jenny. "When will you have some time?" she asked, changing the subject. "I can drive over if Lucas—"

"I'm dying to see you! I have time right now," Jenny rushed on. "But don't you even think about driving over here. I'll be there in—"

Rachel heard muffled conversation in the background, and smiled to herself. She'd forgotten what it was like to need to check with someone about plans.

"Pete needs to come by the Blue Sage to see Lucas," Jenny told her. "And I need to get out of these grubby clothes I've been traveling in. Give us twenty minutes."

"Twenty minutes," Rachel repeated. That would

give her time to change into something less ratty herself.

Jenny's laughter bubbled over the line. "Oh, I can't wait to see you. If I can make it sooner, I will. Don't move from that spot."

Glancing down at her worn jeans and bare feet, Rachel held back a sigh. "I can't wait, either."

When she'd replaced the receiver, she stood, immobilized. She and Jenny had exchanged letters for years. They'd talked on the phone dozens of times, but they'd never actually had the chance to see each other again. The smile on her face slowly grew to a wide grin. Jenny. She was finally going to see Jenny!

Twenty minutes later, showered and changed into clean clothes, Rachel ran the brush through her hair one last time. Hearing the sound of a vehicle nearing the ranch, she tossed the brush on the bureau and turned to race down the stairs. She hadn't felt so giddy since she was a teenager.

In the kitchen, she flew out the door without a coat and down the porch steps to come to a suddenly shy halt in front of the tall dimpled blonde getting out of a red pickup truck.

"Rachel!" Jenny rushed toward her, and Rachel's shyness disappeared.

Throwing her arms around the familiar, old friend, Rachel hugged her. A feeling of peace swept through her at the returned embrace. A peace she had been without since her mother had died.

"Let me look at you," Jenny said, taking a step back and clasping Rachel's hands in hers. "You don't look a bit different, only grown-up. And so pretty." She turned her head to look behind her. "Isn't she pretty, Pete?"

A cowboy next to Harley, who'd emerged from the barn, approached them with a shy smile. "Yeah, but then she's your friend." He slipped his arm around Jenny's shoulder and smiled at Rachel. "She always said you were like the sister she never had. She's been going ninety to nothing since she heard that message."

Jenny gave him an affectionate poke. "You would, too, if you were me," she said, and quickly introduced the two.

Pete released his wife. "Harley says Lucas went into town. I'll go help out in the barn while you two catch up."

Tugging Rachel toward the house, Jenny laughed. "He doesn't know that we'll never catch up. Not in a million years. And you must be freezing out here without a coat."

Rachel hadn't noticed the cold until Jenny mentioned it. Suppressing a shiver, she quickened her steps and followed her into the house. Taking two cups from the cabinet, she filled them with coffee and handed one to Jenny. "Help yourself to a piece of cake. I really need to check on Cody. I haven't see him for a while. He was out helping Harley and Lucas."

Jenny settled at the table. "There's a note here for you. Looks like it's from Lucas."

"A note?" Rachel took the notepad from Jenny and read the bold handwriting, so much like Lucas himself. "Cody has gone into town with Lucas..."

"He has been behaving, hasn't he?" Jenny asked her again.

Rachel avoided her friend's gaze by taking a bite of the cake Jenny had cut for her. "We didn't get off to a good start, but things are better."

"That doesn't surprise me," Jenny said with a soft

chuckle. "Lucas is a bit…brusque. Almost to the point of being rude. But he doesn't mean to be that way. When I first met him, I thought he was the biggest, meanest sourpuss I'd ever met. Then Pete's appendix ruptured. Lucas was the first one to help. He stayed at the hospital with me and held my hand during the surgery. After we knew Pete was out of danger, Lucas took care of the ranch. I couldn't have gotten through it without him."

Thoughtful, Rachel nodded. That sounded like the Lucas she had come to know since her arrival. She also understood that he would have sent her on her way that first night, but the approaching storm had swayed him into opening his home to her and her son.

"I don't know what I would have done without him," Rachel admitted. "But I can't stay any longer." She hated asking anyone, even a close friend, for a favor, but until she could feel safe and could get on her feet again financially, she was left with no other choice. "I was hoping Cody and I could stay with you and Pete."

Jenny reached across the table and took her hands. "Of course you can. We may not have grown up together, but you're like a sister to me."

"I don't know how to thank you," Rachel said with a smile of relief.

Jenny tilted her head and studied her. "What's going on, Rache? You never mentioned you were planning to visit. That's not like you."

Rachel's smiled wobbled. "I'd hoped I wouldn't have to drag you into this." She took a deep breath, knowing she had to tell Jenny, before she could accept her hospitality. "Phyllis and Edward are trying to take Cody from me."

Jenny stared at her. "That's ridiculous. Why would they want to do that?"

"They don't believe I can provide a stable home. They think I'm an unfit mother."

Jenny gave an unladylike snort. "That's even more ridiculous. How long has this been going on?"

"For about eighteen months." Unshed tears threatened, but Rachel wouldn't allow them to spill. "They started hinting broadly about six months after Steven's death. Cody and I moved to Pittsburgh, but they had us followed. While we were married, Steven wouldn't let me finish school or let me work, so when he died, the only jobs I could get didn't pay much. I waited tables, mostly, then found a second job. That's when the trouble began."

"I remember you writing to tell me about how stubborn Steven was and how hard it's been since his death," Jenny replied. "I wish you'd told me about his family, Rache. But lots of single mothers have to work two jobs. And his parents could've helped. If not, they could've been understanding."

Rachel nodded. "Yes, but that isn't the way they are."

"Working two jobs doesn't mean you're an unfit mother," Jenny pointed out.

"It wasn't that, exactly," Rachel admitted, avoiding eye contact. "It was the job, itself. I worked someplace that, well, it wasn't acceptable to them." Before Jenny could ask, Rachel hurried on. "We couldn't live in the lap of luxury, but we weren't destitute. They became more persistent, and we kept moving, hoping they'd give up looking. I don't want to involve you and Pete, but coming here was my last hope."

Jenny studied her, her mouth drawn down in concern. "Steven didn't leave you anything?"

"No."

Pressing her lips together, Jenny nodded. "They don't know you're here?"

"Not yet." Rachel glanced down at the hand gripping hers. "But it won't be long. I'm pretty certain they know I'm in the area. The sheriff was here asking questions a few days ago. Lucas helped me dodge them, but I'm sure the man suspects something."

"Did you tell him you were here to visit me?"

Rachel shook her head. "And Lucas assured me he wouldn't give anyone any information."

After giving Rachel's hand a reassuring squeeze, Jenny stood. "You'll be safe with us. We won't let them do this to you."

Rachel looked up to see the door open. Cody walked in ahead of Lucas, both of them trailing wet footprints. When Cody stopped to stare at Jenny, Rachel motioned for him to come to her. "Cody, this is Jenny."

Surprise widening his eyes, Cody stood still and stared. Jenny took matters into her own hands and rushed to him. She pulled him into her arms and picked him up, giving him a loud kiss on his cheek before setting him back on his feet. "It's about time you got here, young man."

Cody's gaze traveled from her western boots to the top of her head, where he had to tip his head back to see. "We came to visit you, but you were gone, so we're staying here." He looked behind him to be rewarded with a smile from Lucas.

Rachel dared a glance at the man who stood smiling at her son. Her heart twisted at the light in Lucas's eyes. She hadn't realized until that moment how much he cared about her son. Miserable at the memory of the words she had flung at him in the barn, she couldn't speak.

"You're still coming to visit," Jenny told Cody, "as soon as your mom can get you packed up."

"I can ride a horse," Cody announced with glowing pride. "Lucas has been teaching me."

Lucas rested a hand on the boy's shoulder. "He's doing great."

"I bet Pete can find the perfect horse for you at our place," Jenny said, tossing a wink over her shoulder at Rachel.

"I have a horse here," Cody announced, a stubborn glint shining in his eyes.

"And I'm sure you can visit Lucas as often as you like." Jenny looked up at Lucas, then turned a questioning expression on Rachel.

"I'll visit *you*." Cody walked from the kitchen, while the others stared after him.

The two women's attention turned to Lucas when he cleared his throat. "Guess he likes it here."

The look he gave Rachel was full of questions she couldn't answer. Unable to think under his gaze, she picked up her coffee cup and took it to the sink to pour out the dark brew. The color was like looking into Lucas's eyes, and her hand shook.

"You and Pete probably need some time to rest up from your trip," she heard Lucas say in the silence.

Rachel turned back to see Jenny watching her. "Oh, no," Jenny said, waving her hand. "Pete's itching to get some work done."

Wondering if Jenny might be reading something on

her face, Rachel ducked her head. "I'd love your company while I pack, if you have time, Jenny."

"Give me a minute to double-check with Pete, and I'll be right back." Grabbing her coat, Jenny hurried out the door.

Rachel took a deep breath to steady herself, then looked up at Lucas. His gaze was so intense, she had to force herself to speak. "I'll need my car, but the tire—"

"It's fixed."

"Thank you. If it's not too much trouble—I mean, getting it out of the shed."

It was a moment before he answered. "No problem."

They stood staring at one another, until she finally broke the gaze and started for the door leading into the hallway. "I'll just see about—"

With two steps, he was next to her, his fingers wrapped around her arm. "You're sure this is what you want to do right now?"

She glanced at the spot where his touch sent tendrils of heat spiraling through her. Slowly raising her gaze to his, her breath caught at the matching heat in his eyes. "I—I need to find Cody."

Lucas didn't speak, holding her mesmerized for what seemed like an eternity. Finally, he released her. "I'll be outside if you need anything."

She watched him turn and leave, unable to move until the door closed behind him. His presence had heated her, his touch had burned her, and now his absence left her chilled.

Giving herself a hard mental shake, she hurried upstairs. She found Cody in their bedroom, pushing his toy cars along the edge of the braided rug. When he didn't look up at her as she entered the room, she stopped and studied him.

It suddenly hit her how much he'd grown in the past few months. She had been so busy running to keep him safe, she hadn't taken the time to really see him. He must have grown at least two inches in the past six months.

But even more, he had matured. She wondered when it had happened. And why she hadn't noticed.

She eased farther into the room. "I'll get your clothes packed if you'll pack your toys."

Cody's head came up, his hazel eyes wide, but she couldn't read what she saw there. Without a word, he nodded and began picking up his cars and placing them in his backpack.

She left him to his chore and concentrated on her own. In the short time they had been at the Blue Sage, they'd made themselves at home. It took several minutes to gather everything together. Nearly finished packing, she realized she had left some of their things in the laundry room.

"I'll be back," she told Cody over her shoulder.

Downstairs, she set the armful of folded laundry on the table as Jenny came through the kitchen door. "Anything I can do to help?" her friend asked.

"We're almost done. Did Lucas get my car?"

Jenny nodded. "It's outside. He said to give a yell and he'll start it up, so it'll be warm."

Rachel picked up the clothes. "As soon as I pack these, we'll be ready."

"I'll tell Lucas."

Rachel felt her excitement mount as she climbed the stairs. She and Cody would be safe at Jenny's. Not that she hadn't felt safe at the Blue Sage. But she'd had to be on her guard, for the safety of her heart, as well as the safety of her son. That wouldn't be a worry once they were at Jenny's.

"Time to go," she said, breezing into the bedroom. With a glance at the spot where she'd left Cody with his toys, she crossed to the bed. But she stopped when she realized he wasn't there.

"Cody?"

There was no answer.

She placed the pile of clothes on the bed and looked around the room. He was nowhere in sight. "Cody, what are you doing? We need to get going."

When he didn't answer, she stepped into the hall and called for him. There wasn't a sound in the silence of the upper story. A sliver of unease snaked through Rachel as she went from room to room, hoping to find her son engrossed in some activity. Coming up empty-handed, she returned to the kitchen, trying to ignore her panic.

"Have you seen Cody?"

Jenny looked up from the table where she sat with a cup of coffee. "Cody? No. Not since he went upstairs earlier. Why?"

"I can't find him. He's not upstairs." Rachel left the room, too worried to explain more, and fought her fear.

"He's probably down here, somewhere," Jenny said, joining her in the hallway.

Jenny went to search the living room while Rachel hurried to the ranch office. To her dismay and mounting concern, the room was empty. Even under the huge desk.

Jenny met her in the doorway. "No luck?"

Rachel's heart thudded at an alarming rate, and she shook her head, fear ripping away her voice.

"I'll have the men check outside," Jenny offered. "Maybe he went to tell Lucas goodbye."

Taking a deep breath to calm herself, Rachel nodded. There was no reason to get upset, she told herself when she heard her friend leave the house. Cody was probably outside, playing with the dogs or seeing the horses one last time.

But what if he wasn't?

Chapter Seven

Lucas entered the kitchen to find Rachel sitting at the table, her face buried in her hands. The knot in his gut tightened. "What's this about Cody?"

Fear shone in her eyes when she looked up. "He's—he's missing."

Frowning, Lucas approached her. "Jen told me. You checked upstairs?"

"Of course I checked upstairs." She started to stand, but sank quickly to the chair again. "And I checked down here, too."

Lucas noticed how pale Rachel was. Dropping to one knee beside her, he gripped the back of her chair with one hand to keep from pulling her into his arms. "He probably slipped out the front way and went outside. We'll find him."

The door opened and Jenny walked in. "Harley's saddling the horses. Pete's going, too, so I'll stay here with Rachel."

"The horses?" Rachel gasped.

"We'll check around the grounds before we lose light," Lucas explained. "He's probably close by. With three of us searching outside, it won't take long. He can't be far."

Rachel gripped the sleeve of his coat. "Yes, he can. If Phyllis and Edward took him—"

Covering her hands with one of his, Lucas felt the icy chill of her fingers. "They couldn't have gotten on the ranch without someone seeing them."

Tears glistened in her eyes and her chin quivered. "But there's no reason for him to disappear like this. Not on his own."

Lucas glanced at Jenny, then focused his attention on Rachel. He had thought she was the strongest woman he had ever met, but she was crumbling before his eyes. He didn't blame her. Having Cody disappear like this was scaring him, too. When had the boy become so important to him? So special? He looked at Rachel. *When had his mother?*

"Kids'll do all kinds of things," he finally told her, getting to his feet.

On his way out, he motioned for Jenny to join him on the porch. "Do you know what Cody was upset about?" he asked when the door closed behind her.

"He doesn't want to leave and go home with me."

Lucas nodded. "I'd bet my last heifer that's the reason."

"I'll talk to her about it and see what we can do." She turned to open the door, but Lucas stopped her.

"Let me talk to her after we find Cody."

Jenny studied him for a moment, then nodded in agreement and slipped inside the house.

Determined to find Cody, Lucas strode down the porch steps toward Harley, who waited in the yard with the horses. Even though the temperature was low, he was more worried about Rachel than he was Cody. And worried about himself. He shouldn't care so much. They would be leaving in a matter of days.

"Pete's gone to check the east pasture. Where do you want to start?" Harley asked him.

Lucas took the reins and mounted. "You can check the west one and I'll ride on down the road. Maybe he decided to take a walk."

Giving his horse a nudge, he rode away from the house. He felt certain Cody wasn't far away. He had come to understand the boy. And he had come to understand Rachel, too. It was her love for Cody, so much like his own mother's love, that gave her strength.

He knew what Cody was feeling, too. And he knew the boy needed a little time alone. Even though Lucas had had one of the best mothers in the world, he knew what it was like to be a boy without a father. Sometimes a mother needed to let go a little. Cody wouldn't get hurt, not unless he had left the Blue Sage. Lucas was sure he hadn't. The boy wouldn't go far from his mom. The two of them had been like bread and butter for too long. But Cody had tasted the sweetness of freedom since arriving at the ranch, and he wasn't ready to give it up yet.

Lucas thought of the conversation he'd had with Rachel. He would never make a good father, but he could at least give Cody the little bit of freedom he needed for a while longer. If Cody were his son—

As he rode farther, with no sign of Cody, Lucas began to suspect he knew what the boy was up to and where he had gone. He hoped he was right.

He turned back and urged his horse faster. Riding

into the ranch yard, he stopped at the barn and dismounted. He led his sorrel through the door and hustled it into the stall, then started down the long walkway between stalls to the back of the barn.

Coming to a stop at the door to the tack room, Lucas gently pulled the lever and opened the door. He stepped inside the room, half-lit by what daylight was left, and came to a halt. A quick look around told him Cody was nowhere in sight. It didn't surprise him. Cody would find a much better hiding place.

Beyond the tack room was a small storage area where he kept the older equipment, the things he and Harley had used when they were small.

Lucas held his breath and listened at the closed door to the room. Not a sound whispered inside. With as much care as possible, he moved the iron handle up and out of the slot which held it.

He swung the door open and waited for his eyes to adjust to the dark room. "Come on out, Cody," he called softly.

Sounds of movement and soft scuffling could be heard in a corner beside a wooden box that held old saddle blankets. Lucas moved in that direction, feeling his way. Hunkering down to where he was certain Cody was hiding, he kept his voice low and friendly. "Cody, your mom is worried. Why don't you and I have a little talk, and then we'll go on up to the house? She's going to be real happy to see you're okay."

"Don't wanna go."

Lucas smiled to himself. Stubborn sure did run in the family. "You mean you want to let your mom think something's happened to you? That you're hurt? That she might never see you again?"

"She wants me to go to Jenny's with her, and I

don't want to. I want to stay here with you.'' Cody slowly crawled out from behind a packing barrel. ''Can I, Lucas? Can I stay here at the Blue Sage?''

Lucas couldn't answer the question. As much as he had grown to like having Cody at the Blue Sage, it wasn't his place to say yes or no. But the pleading in the little guy's voice caused his chest to constrict, making it difficult to say the only thing he could. ''Your mom loves you, Cody. She needs you.''

When Cody sniffed, Lucas didn't hesitate. Sitting on the cold, concrete floor, he stretched out his legs and pulled the boy onto his lap. ''She *needs* you, son.''

Cody was quiet, as if he were considering the statement. ''I could help you. I'm getting bigger. And I can ride good, too. You said so.''

Lucas chuckled. ''Pete could probably use the help of a big, strong, six-year-old even more. But maybe we can work something out. As long as you go with your mom when she says. What do you say? Is it a deal?''

Lucas had grown accustomed to the darkness and could see Cody's eyebrows drawn together in serious thought. His mouth, so like Rachel's, pulled down in a frown, then his face relaxed in a small smile.

He nodded and took a deep breath. ''Okay. It's a deal. Will you talk to my mom?''

Lucas set the boy on his feet and pulled himself up to stand next to him. ''You bet I will,'' he vowed, taking Cody's small hand in his.

On their way to the house, Cody tugged on Lucas's hand, and gazed up at him. ''I love you, Lucas.''

His throat clogged with emotion, Lucas managed a reply. ''I love you, too, Cody.''

* * *

"Cody! Oh, my baby!" Rachel rushed to the door the moment it opened and she saw her son. Weak with relief, she dropped to her knees, pulled him into her arms and covered his face with kisses. "Thank God you're all right. Where have you been? I've been so worried about you."

When her son mumbled into her shoulder, she held him only far enough away to look into his flushed face, but she couldn't stop her tears from spilling.

"I'm okay, Mom. I was just out in the barn. I was—" He tilted his head up to look at Lucas.

"He was just taking a little time to be by himself," Lucas interjected, when she turned her questioning eyes up at him. "We need to talk, Rachel," he added in a low, quiet voice.

Jenny appeared at her side and gently drew Cody from her arms. "Let's get you out of that coat and cleaned up for some supper," she said, leaving Rachel to stare at Lucas.

Rachel stood, a little unsteady from the relief that had rushed through her at the sight of her son, and attempted a watery smile. "Thank you, Lucas."

Lucas nodded, but didn't move. Rachel wasn't sure what to do as Jenny scooted Cody up to the table and placed a bowl of hot soup in front of him. Adrenaline eased from her system, and exhaustion took its place. She didn't want to collapse in front of Lucas and Jenny. She needed to escape, for just a while, to pull herself together.

"I'm going to get the last of our things," she told them, crossing the kitchen. "When you're finished, Cody, we'll go home with Jenny."

"But I don't want to stay with her!"

Rachel spun around to stare at him. "Cody!"

He ducked his head and looked up from beneath his thick lashes at Jenny. "I'm sorry."

Jenny ruffled his hair and smiled. "It's okay. I understand."

With a quick glance at Lucas, who stood studying her, his mouth set in a grim line, Rachel forced herself to turn for the hallway and the stairs. "I won't be long."

Cody and Jenny's voices faded to nothing, and Rachel took a shuddery breath. Just as she'd feared. Cody had begun to like it too much at the Blue Sage. What six-year-old wouldn't, with Lucas for hero material? But he would feel the same way about Pete, in no time. They needed to get away from the man who had grown to mean more than he should.

And *she* had to get away from Lucas. She had seen changes in him, since they had first arrived. Changes that were becoming more dangerous to her heart each day she spent at the Blue Sage. The man she had thought was cold hid a warmth beneath that chilling exterior. Emotionally scarred, yes, but she couldn't deny that maybe it was the reason she felt so drawn to him. They both had pasts they were trying to forget. They were both trying to heal.

In the room she shared with Cody, Rachel folded her son's last pair of blue jeans, smoothing the wash-softened fabric with still-trembling hands and placing it in the suitcase. Cody had changed, too. She'd noticed how the color had returned to his cheeks, how he had become more extroverted, more...male in the past week. Clean fresh air had done that. But that wasn't all. Just being able to stop running for a short time, to put their troubles on hold for a little while, was a big part of it. If they could hold out for a little longer, things would be just as good for them at Jenny and Pete's. At least for a while. She didn't dare plan too far in advance.

Startled by a knock on the door, Rachel stopped long enough to close the suitcase before she answered it. She had hoped she could avoid a private conversation with Lucas, but luck wasn't on her side. When she opened the door, a familiar wave of heat flooded her at the sight of him.

"I promised Cody I'd talk to you," he said, his expression serious.

He didn't move until she opened the door wider and gestured for him to enter. Once he had stepped inside, the room seemed to shrink, and Rachel noticed her hands trembling. Tucking them behind her, she moved away from him. "About what?"

Shifting from one foot to the other, Lucas avoided looking directly at her. "I know what you think of my parenting skills. And you're right," he hurried to add. "But I'm going to stick my nose in here because I promised Cody I would."

When he seemed to be having trouble forming words, she searched her mind for a way to ease the situation for him. "Cody can be very persuasive."

One corner of his mouth turned up in a smile. "Yeah, he sure can. The thing is…well, I think it might be better for him if you both stayed here for a few more days."

"No," she said, automatically. She didn't need to give this a second thought. Wasn't she just thinking about how she needed to get away from this man, before she lost any more of her heart to him?

The half smile disappeared. "Hear me out, Rachel. You've admitted you've been running from one place to another. Cody is just now getting used to the place, and you're going to drag him off to someplace new.''

Rachel bristled at the implication that she'd ''drag'' her son anywhere. ''We've only done it because—''

''I understand that,'' he interrupted. ''Under the circumstances, I'm sure you felt you had to leave.''

''If I hadn't, I wouldn't have Cody with me now.''

''That may be true. But it's pretty obvious Cody doesn't want to leave.''

It had been obvious to her, too, but there was nothing she could do about it. They had to leave. ''Cody needs to realize that he can't always have or do what he wants.''

Lucas's firm mouth softened. ''You're sounding like a mother.''

''I *am* a mother.''

''And a damned good one. Look, I know you want to do what's best for Cody. I'll do whatever I can to help you.''

She had never noticed how smooth he was. He seemed to know just the right words to sway her. But she couldn't let him do it. ''No. You've helped me more than I ever could have asked.''

He shrugged. ''Then let me help once more. What I'm suggesting is that you and Cody stay here for a few more days. Make some trips to Jen and Pete's to visit. Let Cody get used to them. He's had to get used to me. Why force this on him, all of a sudden? You're safe here. As safe as you'll be there.''

He was right. She suspected part of Cody's problem was just wanting to stay in one place. She had hoped that, once they were at Jenny's, they could begin to make plans to do just that. Still, she couldn't be sure her in-laws weren't right behind them. The sheriff *had* been asking questions only a few days ago.

But where would she rather be if Edward and Phyllis did appear? Lucas was little more than a stranger. Jenny was an old and dear friend. Rachel didn't want to see any of them involved. But she felt safer with Lucas. She had to make a decision.

"I don't want to put you in the position where you're involved in my battles," she told him.

Before she could say any more, he had closed the few feet that separated them. He didn't touch her, but he stood so near her that the scent of him surrounded her. She could feel his warmth, almost hear his heart beating.

"Rachel."

When he lifted his hands as if to touch her, she took a step back. She couldn't risk the contact. His frown told her that he didn't find her retreat to his liking.

"I don't want to involve Jenny, either," she added quickly. "So we'll stay. But only for a few more days."

His shoulders relaxed, and the hard line of his jaw eased as he let out a long breath. "We'll take him over to Pete and Jen's tomorrow. Pete has a horse picked out for him."

She shook her head. She didn't like the way he had suddenly changed her job as mom to "we." "*I'll* take him over tomorrow. I'll leave the things in the trunk, and we'll use what isn't packed. Pete can show him the horse tomorrow, and maybe that will help."

"A little each day," he said, taking a step back. "That's good. Cody'll be able to adjust."

"I don't understand why it matters to you," she blurted when he turned to leave.

He stopped, his hand on the doorknob. A sad, wry smile tilted his mouth. "I'm not the tyrant you think I am, Rachel. I care a great deal."

His gaze moved over her from head to toe and back again, sending a shiver of heat down her spine. It was as if he had left something unspoken. What was it?

"I ought to tell you," he said, after he'd started out the door. "I told Cody he could come visit when he gets settled in at Pete and Jen's. And I intend to visit him, too. I've always been real neighborly with the Richmonds."

The implication hung in the air after he had gone. Rachel hated to admit it would be better for Cody to continue his friendship with Lucas. He was a good, honest and caring man. So unlike Cody's father, who had never had time for his own son.

But staying at the Blue Sage, even for a few days, wasn't good for her heart. The less she saw of Lucas Callahan, the better. The rugged cowboy turned her inside out. The sooner she could take Cody to Jenny's, the sooner she could begin to forget Lucas. Once there, she'd make certain she was busy—and out of sight— when he came for a visit.

Lucas sat at the scarred desk, surrounded by paperwork needing his attention. But he couldn't concentrate. After Jen had left, and Rachel had taken a drooping Cody upstairs for a bath, Harley had ambled into the kitchen. Lucas had given him a quick rundown of his conversation with her.

Harley had agreed that it would be best for Cody if they eased him into the move to Jen and Pete's. Lucas was certain he could keep them safe. What he wasn't certain of was whether he could keep himself safe from his growing feelings for Rachel and the boy. And they wouldn't be staying long. He didn't know how he'd react to having his guests gone, when the time came.

After a call from Ben, he knew the sheriff wasn't having an easy time keeping Rachel's whereabouts under wraps. Whoever was looking for her—and he felt sure it was Cody's grandparents—was getting close. Too close.

Shoving away from the desk, he stood, uncertain of how to help, if they did find Rachel. Losing a child was something he understood, although he had never seen his own. He wouldn't let anyone take Cody from Rachel.

There were things about her he wanted to know for himself. Had she loved her husband? Was she still a grieving widow? Was that what made her keep her distance?

He had known she was trouble from the first moment he'd laid eyes on her. But she hadn't been the kind of trouble he'd expected. He hadn't planned to have to fight off a craving for just the touch of her. It was getting worse by the day, and Lucas didn't know how to fight it anymore.

Restless energy and indecision drew him from the office into the hallway. He heard the quiet opening and closing of cabinets and the ping of metal hitting the sink coming from the kitchen. He was alone in the house with Rachel and Cody. The sleepy-eyed boy wouldn't be in the kitchen this late. It had to be Rachel.

At the doorway, he stopped to watch her fill a teakettle with water, her back to him. Wearing a sweat suit two or three sizes too large for her, she looked like a small child, as vulnerable as the boy who slept upstairs. It only intensified Lucas's need to keep her safe and brought his need to touch her to the boiling point.

She shut off the water and moved on bare feet to the stove, where she set the kettle on the burner, then lit the fire. When she turned, her eyes were downcast, but as she moved across the room to the table, she glanced up.

Her gasp of surprise made him smile. "Late-night snack?" he asked, hoping to calm the wild look in her eyes.

"I—I couldn't sleep. I guess Cody's disappearing act still has me upset."

Lucas stepped into the room, nodding. "He had us all upset."

With her hands clasped in front of her, she lowered her head. "I'm sorry. We didn't mean to be so much trouble."

Exasperated that she would blame herself, Lucas strode toward her, but he stopped before he reached her. Pulling out two chairs at the table, he let out a long breath. "Cody didn't mean to do it."

"No, of course he didn't. He's just a little boy. He doesn't understand." Looking up, her soft smile eased the lines of worry on her face. "But I don't think he'll do it again. I have you to thank for that. You seem to understand him much better than I do."

He waited while she took her place on one of the chairs, then he settled onto the other. Now that he had her attention, it was time to get his questions answered. But he would have to go slow and easy. He didn't want to scare her off.

Clasping his hands on the table in front of him, he

kept his gaze from her. "Kids don't stop to think about what their actions do. They just know what they want and they act."

"And Cody wants to stay here," she said with a sigh. "You're the only man he's been close to for a long time. I can't blame him for wanting some male companionship."

Glancing up, Lucas saw the red stain on her cheeks and wondered if Cody was the only one who wanted male companionship. The urge to reach out and take her hand in his nearly drove him to do it, but the sound of the teakettle whistling brought her to her feet.

While he watched her take a cup and tea bag from the cabinet and pour the steaming water, he thought about how to approach her on the subject of her husband. It was ludicrous that her in-laws would want to take Cody from her. Rachel was the perfect mother, so like his own that his heart ached at the thought. Only a fool would ignore the love she had for her son, and the good care she had taken of him.

Before he could think of the best way to broach the subject, her voice jerked him back to the here and now. "I'm sorry. Can I fix you some tea?"

"I'll do it," he said, getting to his feet. He didn't need the tea, but a cup in his hands would give him something to do. Something to keep him from touching her.

He waited for her to sit again before striding to the cabinet and the tea things. As he poured the water into the cup, he reminded himself that asking her to share her past with him would be opening himself up to questions, too. His life with Debra and the pain it had caused was something he didn't care to share. He had been able to put it from his mind. But the moment

Rachel had climbed out of her car, the wounds had opened again. Until he could cope with it, he wasn't quite sure he was willing to talk about it.

"You lived in Pennsylvania?" he asked once he had returned to his chair.

"Near Philadelphia," she answered after a moment of hesitation. "Steven's parents are very influential there."

Afraid he had scared her into not talking, he didn't know what to say next. Communicating with anyone other than Harley had always been difficult. With his stepbrother, he never needed to voice his emotions. Harley always sensed Lucas's feelings. A part of him wished Harley were there to help him through this.

Knowing the only way to get answers was to ask questions, Lucas took the plunge. "How long were you married?"

Her shoulders stiffened, and her hands clenched the cup she held. When she looked up, her blue eyes shimmered with unshed tears. "Seven years. When we met, I was surprised he was even interested in me. I was barely eighteen, and he was the first man who took any notice of me. I suppose I fell in love with the attention he paid me, as much as I did with him."

The image of a suave, city man formed in Lucas's mind. It was no wonder she hadn't shown more than simple courtesy to a man who had known nothing but ranching and wide-open spaces. Compared to a cosmopolitan, a backwoods rancher wouldn't have a chance. Hadn't he learned that lesson with Debra?

"He was older?" he asked.

"Only by two years. We met my first year in college." She ducked her head. "What little college I had. His world was so different than what I'd known in the foster care system. He was…urbane. Charming. He moved in a circle of wealth that kept me speech-less."

"And you married him," he prodded, thinking of Debra's gold digging.

Her head came up, and she stared at him, her eyes flashing with fire. "You think I married him for his money."

He held her gaze. "Did you?"

Pushing away from the table, she started to rise, then stopped, shaking her head. "No. No, I didn't. His parents might tell you different, but it wasn't his money that attracted me. Oh, I admit, I was in awe of the way they lived, but I never wanted it for myself. All I wanted was to be loved."

He should have been relieved at her admission to not caring about money. Instead, tension built in him, and his gut twisted. "He didn't love you?"

"Only as much as he could," she answered in a whisper. "At first, he showered me with attention, took me to places I'd never dreamed of going, bought me expensive gifts. But that isn't love, is it?"

Her words cut him. He had adored Debra, granted her every wish, even to the point of putting the Blue Sage in financial trouble at one point. But he had loved her. Until he had realized all she'd wanted was money, and the things it could buy. He'd wanted someone like Rachel, just as she had wanted someone like—

"For some people it is," he answered, before his thoughts took him down the wrong path. "But if he had so much money, why are you without now? Hadn't he made provision for you and Cody? Didn't he have life insurance?"

Her smile held a hint of bitterness. "He cashed in

his insurance policy to pay off some of his debts. The little we had left when he died didn't even cover the rest he owed.''

''Why didn't his parents help?''

Silent, she reached for the cup and took a drink before answering. ''They refused to help. They never believed he had a gambling problem. They didn't want to believe he'd do anything wrong. So they blamed me for everything. I never asked him for anything, Lucas,'' she said, leaning closer to him, her eyes bright. ''Except for a baby. He didn't want one.''

''But you had Cody,'' he pointed out, still hoping to see deception in her. He admired too many things about her. There had to be flaws.

Nodding, she sighed, her shoulders slumping. ''Cody was an accident,'' she said, raising her gaze to his. ''As far as Steven was concerned, anyway. For me, he was a miracle. I'd given up hope. If I hadn't become pregnant...if it hadn't been for Cody...''

Lucas watched her duck her head to hide her face. It was plain to see that Cody was her life. And had been for a long time. If only he had been so lucky to have found someone like her, instead of the woman he'd married. Having Cody burst into his life brought renewed mourning for the child he had lost. But Cody also brought a ray of sunshine and laughter that had been missing from his life for years. He hadn't realized how much he'd longed for it, until the day Cody and Rachel arrived. Unfortunately, they would be leaving soon.

He had grown so accustomed to having them around, he didn't know how he'd get along without them. Without her. And, if he was honest, he didn't want to find out.

Getting to his feet, he rounded the table and placed a hand on her shoulder. "You've raised a fine boy," he said, his voice rough with emotion. "Don't you worry about his grandparents taking him. There isn't a court in this country that would let them do that. And neither will I."

While Cody was busy helping Lucas with ranch chores, Rachel had free rein of the house. A pot of stew bubbled on the stove, awaiting the arrival of five hungry men—Cody included—for lunch.

Dinner, Rachel reminded herself. Smiling at the small differences between country and city expressions, she placed the vacuum back in the closet. Beside it, she set the plastic box of cleaning supplies. Lucas might frown at her passion to keep the ranch house sparkling, but in doing so, Rachel found great satisfaction and pride.

And it did sparkle. From the glimmering droplets of the crystal chandelier hanging in the dining room, to the glossy dark woodwork, the old but noble house shined. It pleased her to see the changes she had made. All it had needed was a loving hand to erase the remains of dusty boots and neglect.

She gathered things in the kitchen, then breezed into the ranch office and dropped the mail Lucas had brought in earlier onto the gleaming desktop. Of all the rooms in the house, she liked this one best. The kitchen was warm and friendly, and despite its size, cozy, but the office intrigued her. Pure masculinity, from the rough, wooden paneling to the massive mahogany desk and leather chairs. Although some might find the dark hangings at the windows daunting, she enjoyed the feeling of protection it gave her. In here, nothing could bother her, no one could harm her.

It had been two days since Lucas had assured her no one would take Cody from her, and since then, she had clung to the conviction in his words and voice. Each time she had begun to doubt, she'd returned to the solace of the room.

Sinking into the leather chair, Rachel tipped her head back and closed her eyes. The men wouldn't be returning for a good half hour, and she wanted to savor the silence and solitude. Smiling, she thought of Cody. Ranch life suited him. They had been at the Blue Sage for more than a week, and she had seen her son take on a liveliness he'd never had before. Smiles came more easily, and the wary look had left his eyes. Even his cheeks had taken on a rosy glow. Except for an occasional pout when his desire was thwarted, he had been in the highest of spirits. She hoped his happiness continued to grow, even once they moved on to Jenny and Pete's.

She didn't hear the iron knocker pounding on the front door at first, but when she did, she levered herself from the chair and went to answer it. Visitors rarely stopped at the Blue Sage. Although well-respected by the people in the area, Lucas wasn't overly social. Too busy with ranching, a weekly visit to town for supplies was his only activity. Other than Harley, the hands and Jenny and Pete, the only person who had stopped by to see them had been Ben, and that had been business.

The knocking continued as she reached for the door and opened it, curious to see who the persistent visitor might be. Her gasp froze in her chest when she found herself face-to-face with Edward and Phyllis Harris.

"You might invite us in," Phyllis said, her voice as cold as the weather outside. Edward stood beside her, his face a mask of no emotion other than a slight scowl.

Placing her hand over her heart to assure herself it was still beating, Rachel fervently wished she hadn't bothered to answer the door. How had she been so foolish to think she was safe, even at the Blue Sage?

"Wh-what are you doing here?"

Phyllis's mouth puckered, but it was Edward who spoke. "We've come to see our grandson."

"Really, Rachel," Phyllis said, pushing past her into the hallway, "You didn't think we wouldn't find you, did you?"

Rachel bit back the retort that sprang to her mind. Past experience had taught her that answering would only antagonize the woman. Closing the door after Edward stepped through the doorway to follow his wife, Rachel crossed her arms on her chest and waited for their explanation. Before, she had panicked and run. This time, she was stronger. She wouldn't back down. She had nowhere else to go.

Stepping around them, she led them into the living room, then took their coats and placed them on a chair near the door, determined that the couple wouldn't be staying long. Gesturing toward the sofa, she remained standing.

Phyllis Harris ignored her offer. "What were you thinking, bringing Cody to this godforsaken place?"

"Cody likes it here," Rachel replied, lifting her chin in defiance. "And so do I."

Unlike his wife, Edward lowered himself onto the sofa. "Don't you think you've subjected him to enough strange places?"

"He needs a home," Phyllis said, joining her husband on the sofa. "This gypsy life you've been leading isn't good for him."

Rachel pressed her lips together to keep from telling her that it was their fault she and Cody were running. "We're settling here."

"Here?" Phyllis asked, looking around the room.

"Are you employed?" Edward asked.

"No, not yet. But I know of a place where I can get a job," she answered, thinking of The Rusty Dog.

Phyllis started to speak, but Edward placed his hand on her arm. "And where might that be? In that village we passed through on our way here?"

Rachel hated to tell them anything, but she knew she had to. "In Deerfork."

"Where will you live?"

It was so like Edward to be direct. No pussyfooting around for him. His questions were to the point, and Rachel knew he expected the same of the answers he was given. "I have a place, but I don't feel I need to tell you until we've moved," she hedged, knowing it wouldn't suit him.

Turning to her husband, Phyllis ignored Rachel. "What did I tell you? She's determined to keep Cody away from us. Her secretiveness is only proof that she isn't fit to be his mother. There's no telling where she'll be working or where she'll take Cody. She'll be off again, leading us on another chase." She straightened and looked directly at Rachel. "We won't let you do it. Cody should be in Philadelphia."

Rachel stiffened. "I'm not leaving here."

"Then we'll take Cody with us," Phyllis said, standing. "Where is he?"

Ignoring the question, Rachel walked across the

room to stand behind the high-backed wing chair, hoping the Harrises couldn't see her tremble. She was stronger, yes, but she wasn't prepared to fight them. She had hoped she could get to Jenny's and be settled in before they discovered her whereabouts. But it hadn't happened that way, and she had to remain firm. They wouldn't take Cody from her.

Her fingers gripped the back of the chair as she gathered her resolve. "Cody is staying with me. I'm his mother. He belongs with me."

Shaking his head, Edward stood. "If you'd only agree to give us custody of the boy, we'll see that you have liberal visitation."

"Visitation?" Rachel cried. "He's my son. I've done nothing wrong. You have no reason to take him from me."

"The court can decide that," Edward replied with a shrug.

"They'd decide in my favor."

Phyllis stepped closer. "Don't be so sure. If you won't agree, we're prepared to file a petition immediately. The paperwork is ready. We only need to make a call to our attorney. You'll never be able to give him what we can."

"I can give him love," Rachel insisted, panic rising to cause a tremor in her voice. "I will always provide the necessities. A judge will understand that."

Phyllis's smug smile wavered before she turned her back on Rachel. "A child needs two parents. Not a single mother living with a man."

Before Rachel could find a way to argue the point, Lucas strode into the room. Without hesitating, he walked straight to her and slipped his arm around her waist. The intimate gesture and the feel of him so close brought on a sudden dizziness that a shake of her head couldn't dispel.

Facing her in-laws, his strong, sure voice rang out in the room. "He'll have two parents."

Rachel tried to pull away from him, ready to ask him just how that was going to come about. Was he going to hand her son over to these people? But his strong arm held her tight, pulling her even closer, his fingers digging into her side, silencing her.

"And you are...?" Edward asked.

Lucas reached for Rachel's hand and squeezed it. "The name's Lucas Callahan. Owner of this ranch, and the man Rachel is going to marry."

Chapter Eight

Rachel sagged against him, but Lucas held her snug, defying the couple in front of them to argue. The woman's mouth hung open, and the man's face turned as red as a sunset. But for the moment, neither said anything. Lucas figured he was in for it, from them and from Rachel, but there weren't any other options. He had seen the strange car parked in the yard and had known instantly it was a sure sign of trouble. Once inside the house, he had heard the conversation, and knew he had to do something.

Snapping her mouth closed, the woman bristled, then her eyes narrowed. "This is rather sudden, isn't it? You two could hardly know each other."

Lucas wasn't about to say anything that would get them in any deeper than they already were. These people might have once been Rachel's in-laws, but that didn't warrant them an explanation. "We know each other as well as we need to."

The man leaned forward and looked from Rachel to Lucas. "When is this marriage to take place?"

Cursing himself for not thinking ahead, Lucas looked down at Rachel. Fear and surprise vied with each other in her eyes, but lurking beneath, he saw trust. His heart swelled to the point of aching, with the knowledge.

He attempted a smile, hoping to calm her fear. "We haven't set a date yet."

"You obviously don't know anything about her background," the wife said. "She's not the woman you think she is. She's fooled you, just like she fooled our son. Why, the places she's taken Cody.... Well, it's not the environment for a decent person, let alone a child. But Rachel has never possessed the common sense to know that." Her barbed remark was directed at Rachel with an accusing glare.

Lucas gritted his teeth at the insinuation that Rachel's morals were questionable. Whatever Rachel might have done in the past, he was sure it was for a good reason. She wouldn't put herself or her child in jeopardy. Hell, she had done everything possible to keep them safe and out of the hands of these cold-hearted people.

It took all the manners his mother had taught him, but he managed an answer. "Mrs. Harris, is it? I know her very well. I've seen her with her son, and I know the type of mother she is. Cody couldn't have a better one. I can assure you that nothing immoral has happened in this house, if that's what you're suggesting. She'd never do anything to hurt Cody."

The woman's sniff of a reply accompanied an indignant lift of her chin, but it was her husband who answered. "It seems very clear to me that you're trying to throw up a smoke screen. If you think the mere mention that the two of you will be marrying sometime in the future will send us back to Philadelphia with our minds at ease, think again.''

''Yes,'' his wife agreed. ''You're right, Edward. This does seem to be a story they've concocted in the hopes of deceiving us.'' Her hard stare bore into Lucas. ''That won't happen. *I* can assure you of that.''

''Perhaps you can set a date. We would enjoy attending the wedding, I assure you,'' Edward continued with a smile that didn't reach his eyes.

Pushed to the wall, Lucas searched his mind for a plausible answer. He had been a fool to hope the mention of a wedding would send the Harrises packing. But then, he hadn't been thinking. Now that he was forced to, the idea of marrying Rachel took root. He began to warm to it and hoped, in time, Rachel might, too. But that was for the future, if they were to have one, and he would deal with it, and these sudden feelings, later.

''I've always thought Christmas was a good time for a wedding,'' he finally answered.

''That's well over two months from now,'' Mrs. Harris pointed out. ''Much too far away for Cody's well-being. And since you don't seem to be too certain of even that date, it would be best if Edward and I took Cody back home with us. When and if the two of you marry, we'll discuss the boy's return.''

''No!'' Rachel cried when the woman moved to stand. ''Cody and I won't even be—''

Lucas cut her off. ''We'll have the wedding as soon as arrangements can be made.'' When she started to argue, he held tight to her and hurried on. ''If you and Mr. Harris would like to stay here at the Blue Sage, you're welcome to, for as long as you feel it's necessary. Maybe that will ease your mind about the proprieties,'' he added, pinning Mrs. Harris with a hard glare.

Mr. Harris inclined his head. ''That won't be necessary. We'll find accommodations—''

''I think we should accept Mr. Callahan's offer,'' his wife interrupted. ''If there's room.''

''There is.'' Lucas slipped his arm from Rachel's waist. Gripping her hand to steady her and keep her by his side, he stepped from behind the chair and into the center of the room. The Harrises stood as they approached. ''I'll show you upstairs to a room. While you get settled in, Rachel and I will come to a decision about the date.''

''Lucas, I don't—''

''Now, don't you worry about it, sweetheart,'' he told her, easing her out of the room behind their guests. ''We'll do what's best for all of us. Why don't you wait for me in the office?'' He let go of her and added a little nudge in that direction.

''But—''

''Cody's outside,'' he told them all, but gave her an assuring smile. ''I'll bring him inside and send him up to see his grandparents. We'll get along just fine. Don't you worry.'' At least he hoped so. He could tell by the look on Rachel's face that she wasn't happy about the turn of events. It would take some talking to convince her there weren't any options. Forcing a marriage on her wasn't what he wanted. But now that it was done, he was determined to see it through.

Rachel paced the ranch office while she waited for Lucas to finish with her in-laws and come to explain himself. The peace she usually felt in the room had vanished. It had taken several minutes for her body to cease its trembling. Now that it had, and she had time to review what Lucas had said to the Harrises, her doubts only doubled.

The man had lost his mind. To suggest such a thing as a marriage between them was ludicrous, if not completely insane. What had he been thinking, walking into the room to announce they were getting married? And how in the world would they pull it off, even if she was crazy enough to agree to it?

When the door opened, she spun around to see Lucas entering the room. After shutting the door behind him, he started toward her.

"Hold it right there," she told him, holding up her hand and taking a step back. "If I'd known you were completely insane the first day I arrived, I'd have headed out into that storm. Why, Lucas? What are you trying to do to me?"

Raking his fingers through his hair, he shook his head. "I didn't plan for it to go this way. But when I heard what that woman said about Cody needing two parents, it just seemed right to say we were getting married."

Rachel crossed to the window and lowered herself onto the window seat, burying her face in her hands. "I could have told you it wouldn't work. They aren't the type of people to believe some made-up tale. Now I don't know what we'll do."

"I do."

She raised her head to look at him, and the determination in his eyes frightened her. "Lucas, we can't go through with this, if that's what you're thinking."

"Why not?"

Shooting to her feet, she stared at him. "Why not? You are insane, aren't you?"

In two quick strides he stood in front of her. Catching her shoulders in his hands, he looked down into her eyes. "No, I'm not insane. Think about it, Rachel. You only have three options. You can marry me and get these people out of your hair, you can fight them in court, or you can hand Cody over to them."

His words struck fear in her heart, and she tried to jerk away, but he held her. She raised her gaze to meet his. "No, I won't let them have Cody. I can't."

"Can you afford a legal battle?"

She thought of the meager forty dollars in her purse and shook her head. Maybe in the future she might be able to save enough money to hire an attorney, but not now.

"Would you accept a loan from me?" he asked softly.

Ducking her head, she whispered, "No."

"I didn't think so. That leaves only one option." Tipping her head up, he forced her to look at him. His mouth slanted in a half smile. "I'll admit the announcement came as a surprise to me as much as it must have to you. But now that I've had time to think it through, it makes sense. Perfect sense."

Desire, pure and hot, rippled through her. "I can't marry you," she said as she tried to deny both him and the affect he had on her.

"Is it because of the insinuations that woman made about you?"

Unable to meet his gaze, she lowered her head and nodded, tears burning her eyes. Her job at The Pleasure Palace hadn't been what some people thought. And it wasn't the reason she couldn't marry him. But it was the best she could give him without revealing how she felt.

"Was it illegal?" he asked, his voice low and potent.

She shook her head.

"Was it immoral?"

"Phyllis and Edward think so."

He was quiet for a moment. "Do you?"

Hesitating and wondering what he would ask next, she shook her head.

"Then it wasn't. And it doesn't change anything about what we need to do now. Maybe it would help if I explained." He eased her back down onto the seat, then sat next to her. "The first thing we do is get this wedding thing done." When she started to argue, he hurried on. "Once they see that we're legally married and can provide a good home for Cody, they won't have any leverage in court. I know that. They know that."

She had to agree. It was plain to see that the Blue Sage offered financial security that even the Harrises couldn't argue with and would have to accept. No court would take a child from his mother, if she could provide material needs and a stable family life. With a little time, she could prove they were wrong about the incident at The Pleasure Palace that had been the catalyst for their crusade to take Cody from her. Still, it seemed that she would be marrying him for his money, and she told him so.

"Not from where I stand," he answered. "We can have an agreement drawn up, if that'll put your mind to rest."

The thought of what he'd told her about his ex-wife seeped into her mind. "And yours?"

His nod was brief. "And mine."

"My plans were to go to Jenny's, not bind you to some insane agreement."

He stared straight ahead, his hands clasped between his knees. "You can still go to Jen's when the time is right. As soon as the Harrises are convinced the marriage is for real, and they leave, we can have it quietly annulled. They don't ever need to know."

"Maybe," she answered, still not convinced.

"I'd suggest having someone who isn't legal stand in to perform the ceremony, but I think Edward Harris would pick up on that right away."

"Yes, he would." She sighed. "If only I knew how long we'd have to pretend we were really...married." She turned her head to look at him and noticed a muscle jumping along his hard jaw. "Lucas?"

Stone still beside her, he finally answered, "Yeah?"

She wanted to touch him, to smooth her fingers along his face and ease the tension she saw there. But she couldn't. He was doing so much for her. She wanted to refuse him, for his sake. But she had to think of Cody.

Clasping her hands in her lap, she took a deep breath. "Are you certain about this?"

"I told you I wouldn't let anyone take Cody from you. As far as I can see, this is the only thing we can do. But it's up to you."

She stared at her hands, unable to look at him. His offer of marriage sounded reasonable enough. If they could pull it off, Edward and Phyllis would leave her alone for a while. Maybe long enough for her to find a decent-paying job and save some money in case they tried to take Cody again.

"They'll expect to see Cody, occasionally." She

turned to look at him. "I'll have to let him visit them, or they'll visit here."

"We'll cross that bridge when we come to it. Whatever we have to do, we'll do it."

"They'll eventually learn about the annulment. They've had me followed this far. They're sure to have someone keeping an eye on us. They can't be fooled that easily."

He nodded, but didn't look at her. "For the time being, I think we'd better concentrate on making this legal and convincing them. After they've gone, we'll deal with undoing it."

She swallowed the tears that threatened. How awful could things get? Circumstances forced her to marry a man who didn't love her. Even worse, she had found herself caring more and more for him. His unselfish offer of marriage to keep her from losing her son touched her heart like nothing ever had. And yet, she knew it would come to an end as soon as possible. Then what?

She had no choice. Her son meant too much to her not to risk her heart.

Taking a deep breath, she nodded. "All right."

Lucas turned his head to gaze at her, his dark eyes unreadable. "How soon can we get this wedding thing done?"

"You can't go up there," Harley said, coming down the stairs.

Lucas stopped, his hand on the polished wood of the newel post, one foot on the bottom step. "I need to change my cuff links. These keep hanging up on my coat sleeve."

Harley continued his descent, shaking his head.

"Nope. You can't risk seein' the bride before the weddin'. Bad luck."

Letting out a pent-up nervous breath, Lucas stared at him as he came to a stop at the bottom. "Hell, Harley," he said, keeping his voice low so the guests wouldn't overhear, "it's not like this is a real wedding."

"Reverend Thatcher's here to make sure it is."

Lucas stalled on the technicality. "Okay. It's not a real *marriage*."

Harley's right eyebrow shot up, but he didn't say anything.

Frustration gnawed at Lucas. Nerves had his gut in knots. Did Harley see more than Lucas wanted him to?

Heading back up the stairs, Harley spoke over his shoulder. "I'll get the studs. You get to the office. They'll be comin' down any minute."

Lucas took a deep breath and nodded. Avoiding the small gathering of friends they had invited to witness the ceremony, he entered the office and quietly closed the door behind him.

The silent room was a haven, until his thoughts and feelings caught up with him. He had been outrunning them since the moment he had walked in on Rachel and the Harrises to announce that Cody would have two parents. If anyone were to ask him why he had made that announcement, he'd have told them exactly what he'd told Rachel—it was the only option.

But Lucas knew that if he was honest, he would have to admit there was more to it than that. Much more. In the time it had taken to prepare for the wedding, he had come to realize that he cared for Rachel more than he wanted to admit. The thought of marriage—to her or to anyone—should have had him running for the hills. Instead, he'd been the one to suggest it. And he liked it. The thought of making Rachel his wife brought to life feelings long forgotten and reawakened his heart. So far, he had managed not to think about them. But how long would he be able to keep those feelings at bay?

When Harley entered the room, saving him from dwelling on his thoughts, Lucas took the cuff links and exchanged them for the other pair. Finished, he looked up to see Harley studying him.

"You ready?" Harley asked.

Ready? Yes, he was ready to marry Rachel. Ready to do anything to keep her from losing her son. Ready to play the role of adoring husband. All that was the easy part. It wouldn't take any acting, from him. But when the time came, would he be ready to let her go?

Not wanting to think of what he would have to face in the future, he nodded and stepped into the hallway.

In the living room where the guests had gathered, he took his place beside Reverend Thatcher. Harley stood next to him and gave him an encouraging nod. Lucas realized he had never appreciated his stepbrother more than he did at that moment. They understood each other. Harley had never questioned this plan. And Lucas knew that if he ever needed a friend, Harley would be there. He suspected it wouldn't be long before that happened.

There were so few guests, they hadn't needed extra chairs. The Harrises were seated on the long sofa facing him, with Pete sitting at the end. Ben stood to the right, behind the chair where Terri sat, talking quietly with her. Everyone but the Harrises knew exactly why the wedding was taking place.

The difference between this wedding and his other struck Lucas with a jolt. For years, he hadn't thought about the fancy ceremony in the big church filled with people in Great Falls. Then Rachel had found the pictures. Since then, he'd been able to forget it once again, too intent on the reasons for this one to give it much thought. But now, it came back to him in full force and nearly drove him from the room. His marriage to Debra had been doomed from the first. This one was even more so, since they knew from the beginning it was nothing but a ruse.

Soft voices in the hall drew Lucas's attention in that direction. His gaze immediately went to Rachel, dressed in a cloud of blue. So focused on her angelic face, pinched at the moment with apprehension, he didn't notice Cody wiggle between him and Harley until the boy took his hand. Lucas looked down to see Cody grinning up at him. His heart ached with love for the boy. Giving Cody's hand a squeeze, Lucas winked at him. They hadn't told the boy the truth about the marriage, yet. When his grandparents returned to Philadelphia, Lucas and Rachel planned to explain it to him. Until then, they couldn't risk having Cody unwittingly let anything slip.

Lucas looked up and saw Rachel coming toward him. Indecision and fear shimmered in her eyes. Taking a step forward, he reached out and took her hand. Guiding her to her place next to him, he waited while Jen joined her on the other side, then they turned to face the minister. Lucas wished he could find a way to reassure Rachel that she had made the right decision, but she pulled her icy hand from his and stared straight ahead. He had to focus on getting them both through this. Later, he would deal with the rest.

"Dearly beloved, we are gathered here…"

Rachel prayed no one could see how badly her hands were shaking beneath the bouquet she held. She could barely think past the nerves causing her heart to pound. It was a wonder Lucas couldn't hear the thumping. Were they doing the right thing? Would this really keep Edward and Phyllis from trying to take Cody?

So many questions kept coming at Rachel, she wanted to bury her head somewhere and avoid them all. But she couldn't. What bothered her the most were the lies she had been forced to live to keep one step ahead. She had hoped to end it once she got to Jenny's and had a job. But the deception would have to continue, and now even more people were involved. And she would have to leave Lucas once the marriage was annulled. That would be the hardest.

"Do you, Lucas Raymond Callahan, take this woman to be your lawful, wedded wife?"

Rachel's heartbeat accelerated as she listened to the minister's time-honored words and Lucas's solemn response. Then it was her turn to reply.

"I do," she answered, feeling like the world's biggest fraud.

Lucas took her hand in his, the warmth of his touch giving her some, if only a little, encouragement. He began to repeat his vows, and she knew she ought to raise her eyes to look at him. For the life of her, she couldn't, even when he gave her hand a gentle squeeze.

And then it was her turn. In a voice stronger than she would have imagined possible, she echoed the words of the clergyman, while at the same time, she pushed the guilt to the back of her mind. There was

time for that later. Once the ceremony was over, and
Edward and Phyllis were convinced that Cody had a
stable home with two parents, things would settle
down.

But when Lucas gathered her into his arms for their
first kiss as man and wife, her heart did everything but
settle.

Rachel's eyes widened, and her skin paled for a
moment before flushing bright pink. She laid the pen
on the marriage license where she had signed her
name, and lowered herself onto the nearest chair.
"Why hadn't I realized we'd be sharing a...
bedroom?"

Lucas stood by the office window, wanting to reassure her once again, but not having the vaguest idea
of how to do it. Words were beyond him, and his mind
spun with questions. Was she frightened of him? Or
was she merely frightened of sharing the bed of a man
she didn't know? And she *didn't* know him. Not really. Even he had to admit he hadn't understood himself since the moment she had scrambled out of her
car to face Ben.

Covering her face with her hands, Rachel groaned,
then jerked her head up to stare at him. The pink of
her cheeks deepened to crimson. "I'm so sorry, Lucas.
I didn't mean... Well, you understand my...position."

His attention on her, and torn apart by what to do,
he felt more than saw Harley's gaze. His stepbrother's
nod in her direction forced him to take action. Closing
the distance, he stood beside the chair. The urge to
gather her into his arms nearly drove him insane. But
he couldn't hold her. Instead, he placed a hand on her

shoulder. "Don't worry about it. I'm not insulted, if that's what you're afraid of."

"It's just that—" She shook her head and offered a nervous laugh. "Did you realize that, to make this appear authentic, we'd be...sleeping in the same... room?"

Bed. The same bed. Oh, yes, it had crossed his mind. Day and night. But instead of presenting the situation to her like he should have, so they could deal with it before the fact, he had kept it to himself. Now he had to come to terms with it and help her do the same.

"Yes, once or twice," he admitted in understatement. "There didn't seem to be an appropriate time to bring it up in the last week. We're adults, Rachel. We can deal with it."

Her nod was nearly nonexistent. "Not that we have much of a choice, right?"

She turned to look up at him, and he nearly went to his knees at the panic in her eyes. "Until the Harrises leave, no, we don't. And they won't do that until they're convinced this is a real marriage."

Rachel nodded again, this time with conviction. "Yes. You're right."

Banishing all thoughts of the night that lay ahead of them, he regrettably removed his hand from her shoulder, reminding himself that the slightest physical contact with her would make things more difficult. The reminder only led him to suppress a groan at the irony of his thoughts. His original reaction to her since first seeing her had only intensified, making each day in her company more difficult.

And not only seeing her, but thinking of her. She had crept into his thoughts and dreams, tormenting him with notions of things that could never be. Not for him. Hadn't he learned his lesson about women from Debra?

But Rachel wasn't Debra, and Lucas wasn't sure of anything anymore.

"Maybe we should rejoin our guests," he said in a voice much too gruff.

Rachel glanced at him, then stood, smoothing her hands down the long skirt of her wedding dress. "They'll be wondering what's happened to us. I left Cody talking to Ben Tatum," she said with a nervous laugh as she moved to the door. "He knows not to say anything about all the time we've been on the road, but—"

"Rachel."

She turned back, the picture of confusion and innocence, making her more desirable than ever. His body cried out to close the distance between them and take her into his arms, but he ignored the plea. Giving in would only make things more difficult later.

"There's no reason to hide," he reminded her.

Her eyes clouded, then cleared with understanding. Adding a small smile, she sighed. "We've been running for so long, it doesn't seem real that it's come to an end."

He attempted to offer a smile of his own, but by the look on her face, he knew he'd failed. He wanted her to trust him, completely. But he sensed her feelings for him didn't run as deeply as his did for her.

Without saying anything else, she slipped out the door, closing it softly behind her. He let out a long breath and glanced at his stepbrother.

A worried frown creased Harley's face. "We should've thought about the bedroom thing."

"I did," Lucas admitted after a short hesitation.

Harley caught his gaze and frowned. "But you didn't mention it."

"No. I couldn't risk having her back out of the marriage."

Silence filled the room until Harley spoke again. "Who would that have hurt the most?" he asked, his mouth twitching with a concealed smile.

Lucas squared his shoulders, fortifying himself for the lie he had to tell. "If she'd backed out, she would've eventually lost Cody. This way, they'll be safe from those people." But he knew it wasn't the only reason. He just couldn't let anyone know that. Especially Rachel.

Chapter Nine

Rachel stood in the center of Lucas's bedroom, alone and knowing she shouldn't be nervous. She'd been in the room before, so this wasn't a completely new experience. But it was different. Delivering a stack of clean clothes wasn't at all the same as spending a night together. A wedding night.

She and Lucas had agreed this was the only way. When it was safe to do so, they would have the marriage annulled. There was nothing to be nervous about. Lucas didn't expect anything from her.

But his expectations weren't what worried her. It was her own that made her knees shake and her hands tremble. The man she had just exchanged vows with wasn't just any man. Somehow, he had found his way into her heart. But he didn't know it, and she sensed it wouldn't be wise to tell him. She would just have to find a way to get through this, without letting on how she felt.

Tears came to her eyes as she thought about her

first marriage. It had been a failure, but it had given
her Cody. Now, a twist of fate had brought her to
this—marriage to a man who didn't return her love,
so she could keep her son with her. Failure was in-
evitable this time, too. In fact, they had planned it that
way.

She'd had such hopes on her wedding night with
Steven. Dreams she had never dared to dream as a
child had been within her reach. Family, a home, sta-
bility. But bit by bit, those dreams had been broken
and shattered as Steven's extravagant tastes and care-
less spending had increased, taking over his life. The
repercussions of his actions had reached into hers and
even touched Cody. Since then, she hadn't allowed
herself to dream. Only plan, and hope.

When had she begun to feel at home at the Blue
Sage? Maybe it had come when she had lovingly polished the dark wood of the stairway banister, revealing
the beautiful patina that only time could create. Maybe
it had happened when she had stood at the kitchen
window and watched the sun rise on the rugged Montana landscape glistening with new snow. And maybe
it had been when Lucas's kiss in the barn had brought
together the damaged pieces of her heart.

But if she was honest, it was Lucas, himself. She
had tried so hard to fight her growing feelings for a
man who had closed himself off to everything but
work and a few close friends. Looking back, she
laughed at her first impression of him. She had thought
him hard, but now she realized it was strength built
on a pain she knew little about. She had thought him
cold; but a man who gave his name to keep a woman
he barely knew and her son together had a heart
warmer than any man she had ever known.

Leaving the Blue Sage—leaving Lucas—would be the hardest thing she would ever do. But it would happen. No matter what she felt for him, she couldn't let him know. They were husband and wife in name only. This wedding night would have to be like any other night, in spite of the fact that they would lie together in the same bed. It was a thought she would have to remind herself of more than once during the night, she was certain.

When the door opened behind her, Rachel's nerves and senses came to full attention. Turning slowly when she heard his heavy footsteps on the polished hardwood floor, she prayed Lucas couldn't read her expression.

"They've all gone home," he announced. Crossing the room with his now familiar long strides, he passed by her with little more than a glance and shed the suit coat he had worn for the wedding ceremony.

She turned away when he tossed the coat on a chair and began to unbutton his shirt, but the lines around his mouth and the crease between his eyes stayed in her mind. "Edward and Phyllis?" she asked with nothing better to say.

"They've gone to their room. I think they're beginning to believe this is all real."

But it wasn't. She knew that more than anyone, and the knowledge left her with a dull pain.

"I'm sorry we didn't plan a better honeymoon," Lucas continued when she didn't answer.

"We were too busy with the wedding preparations," she hurried to say. "This way, they'll know we really are..." She prayed he couldn't see the blush heating her face.

"Having a wedding night?" he asked, one inky eyebrow raised.

Unable to comment, she eased to the door. "I—I'll go check on Cody. He's so used to sleeping with me...." Her voice trailed off. She swallowed and breathed deeply. "I mean, he understands about married people sharing a bed, but...I just want to make sure he's all right."

"Rachel?" Lucas said, as she reached for the doorknob.

Instinctively, she looked over her shoulder, but her breath stopped in her lungs, and her heartbeat came to a standstill. On the other side of the room, Lucas stood without his shirt, his previously neat hair in wild disarray as if he had just dragged a hand through it. But it was his tanned body that drew Rachel's attention. Muscles of the type she had only seen in pictures came alive under sun-darkened skin, moving with each breath he took. She had often imagined the strength of his arms, but nothing had prepared her for the reality of a body perfected by physical labor.

"Cody is fine," he said, jolting her with the sound of his voice. "I checked on him before I came in. He's sleeping. I left the night-light on."

"Oh...well...in that case..." She tore her gaze from the bared skin and glanced at every corner of the room, anywhere but at Lucas.

He opened the closet and reached inside, then pulled out a heavy robe. "I'm going to take a shower. I thought you might like some privacy."

She jerked her head around to look at him, again. His dark eyes were unreadable from the distance, and his mouth was set firmly in a straight line. No frown, no smile. She knew he must be thinking something, feeling something, but she didn't know what. Was he regretting his decision, wondering how soon he could be rid of his burden?

"Thanks," was all she could manage to reply, and she moved away from the door. Until she could get control of her pounding heart and trembling body, she needed to keep some distance between them. After all, distance would soon be hard to come by, once they were in the same bed. She prayed he wouldn't notice her reaction to him. She prayed she would be able to sleep with him next to her, so close they would be hard-pressed not to touch.

He strode past her, and she forced herself to stand still, afraid she would either scurry away from him or throw herself against the wall of his muscled chest, hoping he might wrap her in his arms. Neither was the thing to do.

"I won't be long," he said, reaching the door beside her and opening it.

Before she could answer, he was gone, and she was left to stare at the closed door. Her legs nearly gave out as she went to the bureau where she had placed the filmy white negligee Jenny had insisted was the only thing to wear on a wedding night. Opening the drawer, she pulled out the soft folds of the nightie and groaned. What had she been thinking when she had let her friend talk her into something like this? Wearing it, nothing would be left to the imagination. The sheer fabric reminded her of the dancers' costumes at The Pleasure Palace. What would Lucas think, if he knew where she had worked—and where she'd once been forced by circumstances to take her young son?

She shook her head, dismissing the thought, and dug through the drawer, looking for something more appropriate to wear. There was nothing. She had been in such a rush to move her things to his room, she hadn't paid attention to what she had brought. Jenny must have made certain the negligee exchanged bureaus. With a wry smile, Rachel reminded herself to thank her friend.

Hurrying to change and climb into bed before Lucas returned, she kept her ears tuned for the sound of movement in the hallway. She settled against the pillow and pulled the blankets up to her chin to cover herself, her gaze darting around the room without seeing anything. Questions slammed against each other in her mind, and her heart hammered in rhythm with a clock across the room, ticking like a time bomb.

But one question emerged from all the others, loud and clear. How would she ever get through this night?

Lucas turned the shower knob, stopping the stinging, cold spray, and raked his fingers through his dripping hair.

"Hell," he whispered. The word not only described his temperament at the moment, but what his wedding night would amount to.

Taking a deep breath, he rested his forehead against the cold, wet tiles. How had he gotten himself into this mess? He let the air out of his lungs in a long sigh. The answer to his question was simple. He had gotten himself a case of White Knight Syndrome. But even more—and it pained him to admit it—was that he wanted Rachel Harris Callahan with a hunger like none he had ever known. He wanted his *wife*. And he couldn't have her.

She's just a woman, he reminded himself. With a shove at the cold shower wall, he straightened. *Trou-*

ble. One helluva lot of trouble. The thought didn't
change anything. Especially not his feelings for her.
The feelings he wanted to blame on simple lust, but
couldn't.

Dry and wearing a pair of obnoxious-looking boxers
Harley had given him with an equally obnoxious wink,
Lucas pulled on the robe he'd never worn and started
down the hall to the bedroom. He swore under his
breath. He had known he couldn't saunter into the
room the way he was dressed without Rachel knowing
the state he was in, in spite of the cold shower and
the loose-fitting boxers. His mother had given him the
robe as a Christmas gift. He doubted she ever imagined he would use it for the reason he was now. But
besides Rachel, there were the Harrises and Cody to
think of. An encounter in the hallway would certainly
be embarrassing, although it would be proof positive
of how real this wedding night was. Only it wasn't.

Backtracking, he opened the linen closet and pulled
out a blanket. After refolding it into a long rectangle,
he slung it over his shoulder, and proceeded down the
hall.

He paused at the door. The quiet scuffle of bare feet
on wood floor and the dimming of the narrow band of
light beneath the door caught his attention. Rachel had
heard his approach and had turned off the light, probably leaving the bedside lamp on to light his way.
Would she pretend to be asleep to avoid facing him?

Not sure what to expect from her, or himself, he
turned the doorknob and stepped into the room. His
eyes adjusted to the semidarkness, and his attention
went immediately to the bed, where a golden glow fell
over it. Following the mound beneath the handmade
quilt to where the light was brightest, his gaze rested

on Rachel. Her fingers were curled under her chin and gripped at the edge of the blanket. Eyes wide with something akin to fear stared back at him. One look in those eyes, and whatever hidden hope of a real wedding night he might have successfully ignored, vanished. Unfortunately, his desire didn't disappear with it.

He tossed the blanket on the bed and carefully untied his robe. Her eyes lowered, and she pressed her lips together. A small, choked sound escaped her.

"What?" he asked, frowning.

She shook her head. "Nothing." But it came out with a giggle.

Frustrated and confused by her sudden change in attitude, he glared at her. He opened his mouth to demand that she tell him what she found so humorous, but shut it quickly when he realized what was obviously tickling her funny bone.

"Harley gave them to me," he answered with a sigh.

She raised her gaze to his, laughter dancing in her sparkling blue eyes. "Snoopy?"

He didn't usually take too kindly to being the brunt of a joke, but in this case, he would be eternally grateful to his stepbrother for making a strained moment less intense. Maybe it would help. Maybe— No. He couldn't let those kinds of thoughts take him where he knew he couldn't go.

Being careful to keep everything natural and easy, as if this were an everyday occurrence, he finished removing his robe and lowered himself to sit on the opposite side of the bed. He craned his neck to look at her. The covers had slipped lower, and she held them with one hand at her lace-covered breasts. Her

other hand covered her mouth, concealing the smile
he knew hid behind it. Her eyes sparkled, lightening
his heart as his lower body weighted with need. It was
all he could do to keep from reaching for her to tuck
a stray strand of hair away from her face.

"You don't think I'm the Snoopy type?" he asked
instead, his voice husky and rough.

Her hand dropped from her mouth, and her lips
quivered with a restrained smile. "You?"

With her attention diverted, he turned and slipped
under the covers. A rueful chuckle rumbled in his
chest. "No, I guess not."

He hoped he had made his entrance into the bed as
unthreatening as possible, but before he could pull the
blankets higher, she edged away from him.

"Would you like the light out now?" she asked.

Even though she clutched the quilt in a death grip,
he was able to see the smooth skin beneath the lace
of the nightgown she wore. He ached to touch the
softness beneath it, to slide it from her shoulders, inch
by inch, until he could feast his eyes on the satiny
golden glow.

"No," he denied both her question and his
thoughts. She might be his wife—his bride, and this
their wedding night—but it was a marriage in name
only. He couldn't frighten her with his need, fearing
she would run from him the way she had been running
from her past. He didn't want to be her past, too. Not
yet. When the time came for her to leave, he wanted
it to be without strain, without fear.

"No," he repeated, more gently. "Leave it on."
More than anything, he wanted her to relax. Settling
against the headboard, he gathered his strength. "We
jumped into this arrangement without thinking it

through. I take the blame for that. You needed a way to keep Cody with you. I promised to keep you both safe. This was the only way.'' He paused and turned to look at her, hoping she wouldn't agree. Hoping she would say she wanted him, as he wanted her.

She was watching him, an unreadable emotion in her eyes. Their gazes met and held for an instant, then she turned away and nodded. ''And we decided we'd deal with things as they came along.''

''Right.'' He hoped his disappointment didn't show. He'd been a fool to think—to imagine—this night would be special for them. This wasn't the way he wanted to deal with the present situation, but he had learned long ago that no one got everything they wanted.

''This is awkward for both of us,'' he continued, forcing himself to say what had to be said, instead of what he wanted to say. ''We're married, but we agreed it would be in name only, until it was safe to…end it. We don't know when that will be or how long our guests will be staying, but I promise you that you don't have anything to fear from me.'' He couldn't believe the pain saying those words brought him.

He heard her soft breathing, saw the rise and fall of her breasts beneath the blankets. Time seemed to stand still, his promise hanging in the electrified air around them. He had hopes that she might say to hell with the name only part of their agreement. Her silence intensified those hopes, and he found himself holding his breath.

''I'm not afraid.'' Reaching for the lamp beside her, she turned it off, leaving the room in complete darkness.

He wasn't sure what she meant, until he felt her

settle into the bed with a whisper of a sigh, her back to him. Hope died a quick death, but his body didn't get the message. He listened in silence, until her breathing indicated she was asleep, then he carefully reached for the blanket he had tossed to the foot of the bed. Rolling it up, he stuck it between them. Knowing how much he wanted her, he didn't trust himself not to reach for her in his sleep. But it was a long time before he slept.

Sitting at the Richmonds' kitchen table, Jenny took a sip of coffee, put the cup down and looked Rachel square in the eyes. "It's been five days now."

"Right." *Five days and five nights.* Rachel didn't know if she could take any more. She could manage the days. It was the nights that had her ready to do something drastic. And she just wasn't the type to do that.

"So, how's it going?" Jenny asked.

"Everything is working out fine." Rachel hoped her white lie was believable, and added a smile as false as the words to help it along. But she didn't look at her friend.

Jenny's cup hit the table with a thud. "Fine? Is that all?"

The frustration that had built up inside Rachel became too much and burst forth in an exasperated sigh. But even that didn't bring relief. "It's a marriage of convenience. You know that."

"Look at me, Rache," Jenny said, covering Rachel's hand with her own.

Frightened that Jenny would see something in her eyes that would give away her feelings, Rachel hesitated. When she did as instructed, she knew she had been discovered.

"Uh-huh." Jenny's frown softened to a concerned smile. "I kind of figured it was like that. Why don't you do something? After all, you're married. It's not like you're doing anything wrong."

Rachel pulled her hand away and stood. Pacing to the other side of Jenny's kitchen, she shoved her hair away from her face. "Do something? What do you suggest I do?"

"Did you wear that negligee I gave you?"

"Of course I did," Rachel huffed, still pacing. "I didn't have much of a choice that first night. It was either that or nothing."

"Nothing would have been nice," Jenny answered with a hint of something wicked in her voice.

"Nothing wouldn't have made any difference." Embarrassed by the nature of the conversation, but exasperated beyond caring, Rachel stopped and spun around to face her friend. "He made it perfectly clear the first night that he didn't have any intention of making the marriage real."

Jenny stared at her. "Lucas? I don't believe that. He's never been a womanizer, but he's a living, breathing male."

Rachel couldn't disagree with that, especially after seeing him in nothing but a pair of boxers. The memory made her knees weak, and she sank to her chair. "All I know is that he obviously isn't interested."

"Baloney. It must be something you did or said."

"I didn't do anything," Rachel insisted. "He keeps a rolled-up blanket between us."

Jenny's eyebrows raised. "That's it! If you didn't do anything, then he's trying to protect you from him-

self. You have to do something to encourage him,"
Jenny replied with fervor. "Maybe Lucas doesn't realize how you feel." Her gaze rested on Rachel. "You
do love him, don't you?" she asked softly.

Ready to answer in the negative, Rachel stopped
herself. It was time to admit the truth and get the
words out in the open where she could deal with them.
She'd been denying her feelings for too long. Walking
on eggshells had gotten her nothing but a lonely life
without a husband for herself and father for her child.
It was time to take action.

"Yes," she whispered. "Yes," she repeated, louder
this time. "I do love him. And you're right. I should
do something about it."

"Now you're talking," Jenny said with a wide grin.

But Rachel's determination slipped when she
thought of her past. She would have to tell Lucas
about The Pleasure Palace. It was wrong to keep secrets from him, even if telling him might destroy the
future she hoped for. He hated secrets and, sooner or
later, he would find out. She was surprised Edward
and Phyllis hadn't told him themselves. What would
he think of her when he knew? What would he do?
Could she risk it? She had to. After all he'd done for
her, he deserved to know the truth. If it made a difference, and he rejected her, she would have to learn
to live with it. Although how, she didn't know.

Jenny stood and rounded the table. Tugging on Rachel's arm, she pulled her to her feet. "What are you
waiting for? Get going. You can formulate a plan on
your way back to the ranch. Tonight you can put it
into action," she concluded, pushing Rachel toward
the door. "And then you can tell me all about it."

Her warm smile and the sparkle in her eyes gave

Rachel the hope she needed. Maybe it would only take a little encouragement and a lot of honesty to make things right with Lucas.

But once she arrived at the Blue Sage, the plans she had made on the drive were altered. The Harrises' rental car was parked in front of the house, and once inside the door, Rachel could hear voices raised in anticipation coming from the front hallway. She headed in that direction to see what was going on.

"If we've left anything behind, you will send it, won't you, Lucas?" Phyllis Harris was saying when Rachel stepped into the hallway.

"Of course," Lucas answered, his face an unemotional mask.

Phyllis looked up. "Oh, there you are, Rachel. I was afraid we'd miss telling you goodbye."

"You're leaving?" Surprise didn't even begin to describe Rachel's reaction to the news and to the sight of the wide smile on Phyllis's face.

"Yes, we're off. Edward had a call from the executive board, and it seems they've broken the stalemate with one of the corporations he's been dealing with. It's imperative that we leave. He's outside now, getting the car ready." She approached Rachel with outstretched arms and pulled her into an embrace. "But we know that you and Cody are in good hands here."

When Phyllis released her, Rachel glanced over her shoulder at Lucas. His expression hadn't changed. Lips set in a firm line, he neither smiled nor frowned. With his eyelids half-lowered, Rachel couldn't tell what might be behind them.

"I'll take your things out to the car," he announced and picked up two large suitcases. Without a backward glance, he was out the door.

"Of course, we'll want Cody for a visit," Phyllis added as if nothing had happened, "but we'll wait a while, until he's a little more settled into his new life. We can arrange it later."

"Y-yes, of course." Through the window, Rachel could see Lucas loading the bags into the trunk of the car. After shaking Edward's hand, he turned and started for the house, his face hidden by his hat. Instead of stepping onto the wide porch, Lucas turned, heading for the back of the house, and Rachel lost sight of him.

"Now, where's my grandson? Oh, there you are, darling. Come give Grandma a kiss and a hug."

Rachel turned to see Cody standing silently in the doorway. With an encouraging smile, she urged him forward. She watched as Phyllis bent to hug him. Tears sparkled in her mother-in-law's eyes, and Rachel realized how hard it must be for the woman to leave him. Perhaps Phyllis did love Cody for himself, after all, and not as a substitute for Steven.

Straightening, Phyllis sniffed back her tears. "Well, I'd better be going. You know how Edward hates to be kept waiting, especially when there's business to attend to." She took Rachel's hand in hers and held it, her eyes still brimming. "I know it's been difficult these past few months. Perhaps we misunderstood some of the things you did. We never meant to bring you any harm. We only wanted to see that Cody was well taken care of. We're convinced Lucas will be a fine father for Cody."

Rachel nodded, not knowing whether to believe Phyllis or not. It was one more thing Rachel needed to talk over with Lucas.

"If you need anything, Rachel, if something should happen—"

"I'll call you," Rachel promised, giving Phyllis's hand a squeeze before releasing it.

Cody took his grandmother's hand and led her out to the car. Rachel followed in silence, part of her mind wondering where Lucas had gone to. After a somewhat tearful goodbye, she and Cody waved at the car as it disappeared from view down the long drive.

"Can I go help Harley now, Mom?" he asked. "It's my job to feed the new calf."

"That's wonderful," she answered, still distracted. "Yes, of course you can."

She watched Cody, until he was safely to the barn, then she turned, determined to find out where she and Lucas would go from here. This was one bridge they needed to cross now.

The house was much quieter than it had been for over a week. Listening for any sound that might tell her where Lucas was, Rachel prepared herself for the first step of her plan. With Jenny's suggestion in mind, she started up the stairs, but found the second story as silent as the downstairs.

She stepped into the bedroom she and Lucas had shared for the past five nights, and looked around. The room didn't appear to have been touched or even entered since she'd left it earlier that morning, but something wasn't right. She could feel it.

At the bureau, she opened the top drawer. Instead of the collection of silky underthings she expected to see, she found a pile of Lucas's shirts. In the next drawer, where two pairs of her worn jeans had been, there were more shirts. Her heartbeat slowed to a dull thud. Her mind filled with questions.

A hurried trip to the room she had shared with Cody before the wedding proved what she'd hoped wasn't true. Lucas had moved her things back to where they'd come from. But when had he done it? While she had been at Jenny's? He had certainly made quick work of showing her how he felt. It wasn't what she wanted. Not at all.

The truth that he didn't want her stung more than she would have thought. Choking back the tears that threatened to spill and not stop, she wondered what to do next. Getting to Jenny's had been her goal when she had left Ohio, but now that she'd visited her friend, living there for an extended period of time didn't seem right. Jenny and Pete needed their solitude. She knew she and Cody could continue to stay at the Blue Sage for a while longer. Even Lucas wouldn't turn them out if they had nowhere to go, and he would understand about Jenny. If only Rachel could understand him. He looked at her in a way no other man ever had. Because of that, she'd even thought they might have a future together, someday. Had she been wrong? What had made him open his home, but close his heart?

Cleaning out barn stalls wasn't high on Lucas's list of favorite jobs, but the chore left his mind free to roam. Most days, that was good. But not today. He didn't want to think about Rachel leaving. He didn't want to think about Rachel staying. The need not to think twisted his gut. Still, the physical exertion of stall cleaning might take care of his other problem. Cold showers hadn't worked. Maybe working himself to the point of exhaustion would.

The barn door creaked open, creating a swirl of dust

in the stall. Lucas gripped the pitchfork tighter, his fingers aching from the action. He had hoped to avoid Rachel until later. Much later.

"Lucas? You in here?"

His grasp on the tool eased, and he dropped his chin to his chest, blowing out the breath he'd been holding. "Yeah, I'm here."

Harley appeared at the stall door, grinning wide. "Cody sure is gettin' a kick out of that new bull calf."

Lucas grunted in reply and kept pitching the hay.

"I've been thinkin'. What would you think of givin' it to him?"

Lucas couldn't have thought of a better idea, except... "We don't know that Cody'll be staying much longer."

The whisper of hay settling and the rasp of metal on the cement floor echoed in the barn. Harley shifted, his boots scuffling behind the half door. "But I thought that once the Harrises were gone—"

"You thought wrong."

Another moment of silence stretched wide. "You mean you and Rachel didn't...haven't..."

Lucas slammed the tines of the pitchfork against the concrete and pivoted to face his stepbrother. "You know as well as everyone else around here that this marriage was to keep Cody with Rachel, nothing more than to give the Harrises the impression of a happy family. That's *all*. We've done that."

Harley's face flushed red, and his frown became a scowl. "Aw, hell, Lucas, everybody knows you and Rachel are—"

"I did my part at playing White Knight," Lucas said, turning back to his chore. "Rachel and Cody can stay until they feel it's safe to leave." The pain at the thought of them leaving cut deep, and he sucked in a breath, his hands shaking.

Harley hadn't seen the fear in Rachel's eyes. Lucas had. Harley hadn't shared a bed with her, aching with a deep need to reach for her, to stroke her shimmering hair, her satiny skin, bringing her to life. Lucas had. He couldn't do it again. Not another night. The Harrises' departure had at least given him respite from that.

But he would miss her. God, how he'd miss her. The seductive sway of her hips as she moved around the kitchen, the haunting scent of peaches she left behind in a room. The love that shone from her eyes when she gazed at her son. How long would he listen for the soft, musical sound of her voice, once she was gone and the house fell silent?

He'd vowed to keep her and Cody safe. And he had. He would pay the price until the day he died. His promise that she would have nothing to fear from him would be kept, too. Even if it killed him.

"Maybe if you talked to her—"

"There's been enough talk," Lucas growled and flung the pitchfork to the barn floor. He wouldn't discuss his relationship with Rachel—or lack of it. Brushing past Harley, he started for the house. He would be safe in the office. He could put his mind to immunization records and feed prices, and forget about the woman who troubled his mind, day and night.

Trouble. Nothing but trouble.

Chapter Ten

Rachel crept down the stairs and into the office. Curling up in the big chair, she let the comforting smell and soothing feel of old leather surround her. It did nothing to stop the loneliness that was slowly consuming her.

Life had brought her so much unhappiness and instability for so long, she should have been used to it. If it hadn't been for Cody, she couldn't have gone on. Her parents' deaths when she was only seven, and a childhood of foster families and feeling alone were things she'd hoped to overcome when she had married Steven. But that once happy union that had begun as a fairy tale had quickly become a nightmare, ending in even more tragedy. She had become a single mother on the run with her child, broke and afraid of everyone and everything.

And then she'd found herself here, at the Blue Sage, where safety had seemed as easy and natural as breathing.

Lucas didn't like secrets, but there were secrets here. He had his demons, too. She'd tell him hers, because she owed him that much. It wouldn't change things, or the way he felt about her, but she had to tell him. If only she knew what his secrets were, she might be able to understand why he kept his heart locked away. He had given her son the love Cody needed so badly, but when it came to her, Lucas closed himself off and kept his distance. Just as he'd done in the bed they had shared.

Determined to find out what haunted him, Rachel pushed herself to her feet and began to look for the scrapbook. Maybe it held the key to knowing Lucas.

The book lay wedged in the middle of a pile of magazines on a bottom bookshelf. Tugging it free, Rachel returned with it to the chair and opened it, hoping to fit together the elusive information the various pictures and clippings offered her.

"Rachel?"

Startled, she nearly bolted from the chair at the sound of her name, so engrossed in her detective work that she hadn't heard the door open. Until that moment, she hadn't noticed her tears, streaking their way down her cheeks to leave damp spots on her shirt. Realizing it, she brushed them away with the back of her hand. She closed the scrapbook with care and slipped it between the cushion and the chair.

"What is it, Lucas?" She feared the tremor in her voice would give her away, and she tried for a smile.

In less than a second, he tugged her from the chair and had her in his arms. "What's wrong?" he asked, his voice a husky whisper. "Why are you crying?"

The picture of his first wedding blazed in her mind, intensifying her suspicions that the event or those that followed were at the root of his troubles. "Tell me about her, Lucas. Tell me about your wife."

As quickly as he had embraced her, he jerked away. "There's nothing to tell."

She reached out to touch him, but he sidestepped, avoiding the contact. Dropping her hand, she took a deep breath. His pain was evident in his clenched jaw and fisted hands. Somehow, she had to find a way to help him. She had admitted her love for him to herself and to Jenny. Admitting it to him wouldn't change things, but if she could show him a way out of his pain, someday he could give his heart to someone.

Wanting to close the distance between them, she checked herself and stood still. "I need to know. Please."

The muscles in his back and shoulders moved beneath his shirt as he clenched and unclenched his fists. Tension stretched the fabric until, at last, he stopped, opening his hands at his sides. When he turned back to her, despair deepened his eyes.

"It's not a pretty story, but it's time you knew the truth."

The tight feeling in Rachel's chest eased. She nodded and returned to the chair, but sat on the leather-covered hassock nearby instead, hoping he would choose to sit beside her.

He didn't. Pacing the length of the room, the tension returning to his face where his eyes had darkened to near black, he began speaking, haltingly at first. "I thought she loved me, but it was money she loved. She'd have had to be deaf and blind not to see that the Blue Sage was one of the biggest spreads around and one of the few making a profit. Harley warned me, but I wouldn't listen."

"But you loved her."

Stopping for a moment to look at her, he shrugged. "Maybe. I was nothing but a green kid. I'd lost my mother barely a year before that. Maybe I was just looking for a woman's attention."

Rachel had made a mental note of the date of Marie Claire's death while looking through the scrapbook. Although she'd only been a child when her own mother died, Rachel understood his loneliness. "Losses like that are difficult. They can take years to overcome."

He looked at her. "You'd know about that."

His potent gaze made her want to squirm, and she turned the conversation back to him. "How long were you married?" She'd asked before, but she hoped now that he had opened up, he would continue.

"Nearly five years," he answered, resuming his pacing. "Five long years. We were on our honeymoon when she met up with a group of people who were born to money." He came to a halt beside the chair, his mouth slanted in a quirky smile. "I guess you'd know about that, too. And the fast life they lived."

"I have a pretty good idea."

"But you didn't choose to live like that, did you?"

"No. Steven lived life in the fast lane by himself."

Lucas nodded. "Yeah, I didn't join in, either. Maybe if I had…" Running a hand through his hair, he frowned, and the lines in his face deepened. "It killed him, didn't it?"

Rachel nodded. "A car accident. He was running from the authorities. But you were telling me about your wife," she coaxed.

He hesitated before continuing. "We didn't spend a lot of time together, but it was enough. In spite of all of her methods to keep from getting pregnant, we found ourselves expecting a baby.''

''You didn't want one?''

''*She* didn't want it. I'll admit I was hesitant, seeing how our marriage was going, but I'd hoped it would change her.'' His laugh was reminiscent of the one he had given the day Rachel had first found the scrapbook. ''I couldn't have been more wrong. She didn't eat, drank too much and played to the point of exhaustion. I tried to make her see reason, tried to make her listen to the doctor. She had problems with the pregnancy, and he insisted she stay in bed. She ignored his warnings and went on a ski trip.''

A shiver of foreboding crept up Rachel's spine. ''She lost the baby,'' she said in a whisper, not meaning to be heard.

The room seemed to shrink in the silence that followed, until Lucas spoke. ''Yes. And she didn't care.''

Rachel hadn't realized she'd risen, until she stood beside him, her hand on his arm. ''I'm so sorry, Lucas.''

He moved away, his eyes hard and cold, but the anguish in his voice was clear. ''She didn't care that she'd put an end to the life she carried. I couldn't forgive her for that. I couldn't forgive myself for believing in something as foolish as love.''

''Loving someone isn't foolish, Lucas.''

''Isn't it?'' He walked stiffly to the door and put his hand on the knob. ''I wanted to be a better father than mine had been. I tried to be a good husband. I tried so damn hard. But I wasn't good enough, and I never will be.''

''You're wrong! Look at the way you and Cody have taken to each other,'' Rachel argued. ''He cares about you. He loves you. And I think you love him, too,'' she added softly.

Lucas stared across the room as if he hadn't heard her. ''He…our son…*my* son…if he'd lived, he would have been a little older than Cody. If only I'd have had my son. That's all I wanted.''

Realization hit Rachel like an explosion. He didn't love her son. In Lucas's heart, Cody had taken the place of the child he had lost, just as Phyllis and Edward had wanted Cody to replace Steven. Although grief had led Lucas to it, it didn't excuse it. He wasn't the unselfish man she had once thought. It had been because of Cody, all along. How could she have been so wrong?

Before she could find the words to answer, Lucas was gone, leaving her standing in the middle of the room. Silence wrapped around her like a protective shield. She couldn't stay and risk Cody getting hurt. He hadn't been born to replace anyone. Nor could she stay and get hurt more herself.

''Damn, Lucas, you'd have more'n that little pile of chips in front of you if you paid more 'ttention to the cards in your hand.''

The sound of his name being spoken brought Lucas back to the present. ''You say something, Ned?''

The cowboy across the table tossed down his poker hand and snorted. ''You ain't been in this game all day. Takes all the fun outa beatin' ya.''

Harley, sitting next to Lucas, gathered the cards and started shuffling. ''If you'da thought about it, Ned, you'd have known better than to plan an all day poker game this soon after the weddin'.''

A wide grin spread across Ned's face. ''It don't

have nothin' to do with that new bride of yours, does it, Lucas?''

Lucas hadn't felt right since he'd left Rachel in the office a couple of hours earlier. Something kept gnawing at him, but he couldn't put a finger on it. Her questions had come out of the blue, and the force with which they had hit him—the feelings they had brought to the surface—had been too much for him. He'd thought the poker game would take his mind off it. But Ned was right. He hadn't had his head in the game. Or his heart.

"I'm surprised the little lady let you out of the house," Ned said with a laugh. "But maybe she had plans of her own."

Lucas shot him a glare across the table. Even though the marriage wasn't real, Rachel wasn't the type of woman to tell her husband what he could or could not do. And she wasn't the type to run off and share all her free time with her friends, instead of her husband, either. She wasn't like Debra. He'd known that, even from the beginning. If only he'd told her how he felt. But he'd been a coward.

With a hard shove that shook the table, Lucas got to his feet. "The only plans Rachel had were to wait up until I got home," he said, hoping it was the truth. "And maybe that's where I oughta be."

Harley shot him a devilish grin as Lucas counted out the change he owed for the game. When Lucas grabbed his hat and coat, Harley met him at the door. "Looks like you've come to your senses."

"You can tell me later what a damn fool I've been," Lucas told him. "Right now, I have something to tell Rachel."

In his pickup, Lucas felt hope and excitement build.

The tires couldn't spin fast enough. He wanted to be home. Rachel's presence had made the Blue Sage the kind of home it had once been, before Debra, before his mother died. It wasn't just the cleaning and polishing, although Lucas hadn't missed noticing that. It was the sunshine Rachel brought with her into a room that had made the difference. The love she had for her son. The warmth she brought to the heart of a man who had given up on love long ago.

Lucas bumped down the long drive leading to the ranch, oblivious to the late-afternoon sun. With his mind on what he wanted to say to Rachel, he swung into the ranch yard, bounded from the truck and took the porch steps in one leap.

"Rachel!" he shouted in the entryway.

Silence answered him.

Calling her name and Cody's, he searched the downstairs, and then moved on to the top floor when he didn't find her. But she wasn't in any of the rooms upstairs, either.

"Hell," he muttered, returning to the kitchen. She had probably gotten bored and gone to see Jenny, or into Deerfork.

Disappointed, he pulled a cup from the cabinet and poured himself some coffee, hoping it would calm his nerves. The pot had gone cold, so he placed the cup in the microwave to heat it. While he waited, he decided the only good thing he could see about her not being home was that it gave him a little extra time to sort through things and decide exactly what he wanted to say to her.

He loved her. He wanted her to stay. How difficult was that? But would it be enough?

When the coffee was hot, he settled at the table and

reached for a pencil. Grabbing the pad they kept for jotting down notes and lists, he started to tear off the first sheet of paper. He stopped in mid-rip. Rachel's feminine handwriting jumped out at him. Thinking she'd left a note to let him know where she had gone, he began reading, quickly at first, until he realized what it said.

Lucas,

Thank you for taking care of Cody and me when we needed someone the most. Now that Edward and Phyllis have gone back to Pennsylvania, it's time for us to move on. I'm sure we'll be safe now. As soon as we're settled, I'll contact a lawyer about the annulment and have him get in touch with you.

We'll never forget what you've done for us.

Rachel

Lucas stared at the paper, unable to believe the words. His head pounded, and his heart raced. No. *No!* She wouldn't leave without talking to him about it. He had opened his heart to tell her about Debra. Hadn't she understood?

But how could she have known that he loved her, when he only just admitted it to himself?

With a wounded cry, he raced up the stairs to her room and found everything as neat and clean as always. But the drawers and closet were empty. Cody's backpack no longer hung from the back of the doorknob. Her shoes weren't by the chair facing the window.

She and Cody were gone. And he had to find them. His mind racing with the words he needed to say,

he drove to Jen's. Rachel and Cody had nowhere else
to go, and even if they did, Rachel wouldn't take off
without saying goodbye to her friend.

"You know where she is, Jen," Lucas insisted,
standing in the Richmonds' kitchen. His frustration
with the woman's pussyfooting answers to his questions had him tied up in knots.

She shook her head, her eyes brimming with con-
trition. "I can't. I promised her I wouldn't."

"If you care about her, you'll tell me." When Jen
didn't answer and refused to look at him, Lucas's
hopes hit bottom. Had he ruined everything with his
stubborn pride? "I've got to find her and tell her how
I feel, Jen."

Her sigh left him with no hope. Silent for a moment,
her face suddenly brightened. "I can tell you this
much. She has to take care of some *bills*."

"Bills?" Lucas stared at her, baffled by the statement. What bills did Rachel have? "What are you
talking about?"

Chewing on her bottom lip, Jen shifted from one
foot to the other. "You know. She's gone to…see
about the statements. She has to get money to pay
them. You know. A job."

Lucas shook his head. The woman wasn't helping.
"I'll find her without your help," he growled, turning
on his heel and making his way to the door. Suddenly,
he stopped.

"*Bills*. Rachel's going to *Billings*."

"Yes!" Jenny cried.

He quickly thanked her, not wanting to lose any
more time. When he caught up with Rachel, he'd be
sure to tell her how trustworthy Jen had been.

He'd driven for more than an hour when a quick

look at his gas gauge sent him searching for a service station. At the first one he found, he stopped and fidgeted, while the aged attendant filled the fuel tank. It took all the control Lucas could gather not to grab the nozzle and do the job himself.

"Where ya headed?"

"Billings," Lucas answered, pacing at the side of the truck.

The man turned clear, blue eyes on him. "You in a hurry?"

Not in any mood for small talk, Lucas growled an answer. "I'm looking for my—" He swallowed the rest of the explanation and gazed at the golden ball of fire setting in the western sky. "I'm trying to catch up with a woman. I don't suppose you've seen a ten-year-old, red Mustang go by here this evening."

Scratching at two days' worth of beard, the man squinted. "Well, now, there was a lady come through here, oh, 'bout half an hour ago. Had a little boy with her."

"That's got to be her!" Lucas's heart thundered as he reached for his wallet and pulled out a fifty-dollar bill. He handed it to the man, then took the nozzle from him and slammed it onto the tank. Jerking open the pickup door, he turned to the man. "A half hour, you say?"

"'Bout that," the old man said, nodding.

"Thanks. Keep the change." His heart hammering with anticipation, Lucas pulled away from the pump, tires spewing gravel in a dusty cloud behind the truck.

The miles ticked away, leaving Lucas with time to think. With his thoughts came worry. Worry that Rachel didn't come close to feeling for him the way he felt about her. Worry that, if he didn't find her soon,

she would look for a place off the interstate to spend
the night. But he vowed that if he had to check every
off-ramp all the way to Billings, he would find her,
no matter how long it took.

Driving past a truck stop tucked away on the side
of the highway, Lucas nearly missed seeing the red
Mustang. Backtracking some fifty yards, Lucas attempted to calm himself as sweat broke out on his
forehead and his hands stuck to the steering wheel.

She could send him on his way. He might have
mistaken her kindness and soft heart for something
more. Maybe she only felt pity for him. Except for the
one kiss they had shared in the barn and the other on
their wedding day, they had rarely touched, though
he'd ached with wanting to hold her close more times
than he could count.

By the time he'd parked where he could see the
diner's exit, he knew he would do anything to keep
Rachel with him. He would agree to anything, even if
it meant starting over. But no matter what, he'd take
her back to the Blue Sage and someday make her his
wife in more than name only.

He didn't have to wait long before the glass-and-
chrome door of the truck stop diner swung open to
release Cody and Rachel. She looked beautiful. The
sun, its final edge ready to dip beneath the horizon, lit
her hair with reds and golds. This was the woman he
hoped to spend the rest of his life with, if only he was
given the chance.

Praying he would say the right thing, and that she
would listen to him, he climbed from the truck and
eased the door closed. Gravel crunched beneath his
boots as his footsteps brought him closer to the woman
and boy he had come to love. Neither of them seemed

aware of his presence, so he stopped at the rear of a pickup and waited. They would have to pass him to get to their car.

Cody spied him first, letting out a cry of delight and launching himself into Lucas's arms. "I knew I'd see you again!" the boy crowed. "I told Mom you'd come find us."

"And I have," Lucas said, but his attention was on Rachel.

Walking toward them, her mouth was set in a firm frown. Creases marred her usually smooth skin which now was pale and strained. She looked tired, more beat than she had looked the first time he had seen her.

Lucas leaned to whisper in Cody's ear. "I need you to do something for me, Cody. I'm going to give you some money, and I want you to go back inside the diner and get yourself some ice cream. Can you do that?"

Cody's arms tightened around his neck. "You aren't going to leave, are you? You'll take us back home, won't you?"

Home. The word warmed Lucas's heart. "We'll be going home soon," he assured Cody, setting him on his feet. "But I need to talk to your mom."

Lucas slipped a five-dollar bill into Cody's hand and the boy turned and nearly collided with his mother on his way to his dessert.

"Cody?" Rachel turned to watch him.

"He's just going to have some ice cream," Lucas explained. Hesitant, he took a step forward. "Why did you leave?"

Facing him, Rachel tugged at the hem of her shirt. "It's time. Jenny has a friend who'll help me find a job and put us up for a while, until I can find a home."

"You have a home at the Blue Sage."

She couldn't meet his gaze. "That was only a temporary arrangement."

Lucas couldn't stand the distance between them. The need to touch her was more than he could bear. He closed the few feet that separated them, but instead of reaching for her, he stuffed his hands in his pockets. "It could be permanent."

Glancing at him, she shook her head. "Cody needs a stable life."

"And running again is stable?"

"No, of course not, but, I plan to settle down, now that I'm sure Edward and Phyllis won't try to take Cody."

Lucas had been determined to take the bull by the horns, but looking at Rachel, he knew he would have to tread carefully. They needed to work some things out before they could return to the ranch. If he told her how he felt now, he was convinced he'd only frighten her and send her running again.

"Who's to say Phyllis and Edward won't try to take him?" he asked.

Rachel bit her bottom lip. "Nobody, I suppose." She looked up at him, her smile, like her eyes, sad and full of regret. "I guess we'll cross that bridge when we come it. You won't tell them I've left, will you?"

The question was like a punch, leaving Lucas reeling. Did she think he was that heartless? The realization that she might made him dizzy. Stepping back to lean against the tailgate behind him, he tugged his hat lower. "I don't plan to tell them anything, but I do think you should come back with me. You and Cody. After a while, the Harrises will be convinced that all's well. We don't want to take a risk where they're concerned.''

Her shoulders drooped in relief and Rachel gave him a weak smile. "Thank you for offering, but we'll manage fine. You don't know how grateful I am to you for helping us. Edward and Phyllis would still be here or maybe have Cody if…well…"

"If we hadn't shown them what a happy, loving family we are?"

"Yes," she agreed quickly. "And I understand that you only offered marriage to help us. You'll never know what that means to me. But I can't hold you to it any longer."

If he hadn't known better, Lucas would have believed she meant every word, but the sparkle of tears in her eyes told him she was lying. He had known only one other woman who could match Rachel for strength and generosity. His mother had given up her own needs and wants, many times, for his happiness and her husband's. But his father had been weak and selfish, leaving a loving wife and young son to fend for themselves. Lucas hadn't inherited the weakness, and he didn't know how he could possibly live without Rachel. Did that make him selfish?

"Doesn't it matter that I love you?" he asked.

Behind her, the sun shot its last rays of fiery red across the wide sky in a blaze of beauty only equaled by Rachel. Like the sky, she remained silent.

Lucas shoved away from the truck and approached her, tilting her chin with a finger and forcing her to meet his gaze. "I can give you the permanence you and Cody are looking for. I need to give you that. Without the two of you, I'm lost."

Her eyes searched his, their blue depths pulling him

deeper, until she sighed. "Cody isn't a replacement for the son you lost," she whispered.

"A replacement for—" Lucas couldn't believe what he was hearing. "Is that what you think?"

Turning her head away from him, she nodded.

He put his hands on her shoulders and pulled her closer. "Cody could never be the son I was cheated of. I wouldn't want him to be. I love Cody, but I love him because of who he is, not who he might represent." Wrapping her in his arms, he held her tightly. "And I love you, Rachel. Come home with me."

She leaned back to look up at him, tears shimmering in her eyes. "I thought it was because you wanted Cody to be the son you'd lost. That you didn't want us, that you didn't want me. All those nights—"

"All those nights were a long journey in hell. But I'll make them up to you, every one of them, if you'll only come home. Please, Rachel."

When she shook her head, he nearly died. He couldn't lose her.

"There's something I need to tell you," she said, before he could form the words to convince her of his love. Her eyes filled with apprehension. "The job in Pittsburgh, the one Phyllis and Edward objected to—"

"Whatever it was, it doesn't matter." He didn't need to hear about her past. It was the future he cared about. "I love you, Rachel, no matter what."

Bright spots of red colored her cheeks. "I have to tell you, Lucas."

He didn't doubt her morals or her reasons for doing what she had to do, but he sensed the strength of her need to bare her soul. "Then tell me."

Her small nod tugged at his heart. "I was employed at a place called The Pleasure Palace."

"A strip bar?" he guessed. "You were a stripper?"

"No! I wasn't a—a dancer." Her face flooded with color. "I was the seamstress for the exotic dancers there. I made their costumes."

Her admission stopped him cold and nearly caused him to laugh. "A seamstress? And you're ashamed of that? Don't you know, it wouldn't matter to me what you did?"

She shook her head, as if his acceptance were wrong. "That's not all. One day, Cody's baby-sitter couldn't watch him. I had to take him to the club with me. I couldn't leave him home alone. I kept him in the office. I swear he wasn't anywhere else. But Phyllis and Edward said it was wrong. A good mother wouldn't take her son to a place like that. But I needed the money, Lucas. I swear, I wouldn't have—"

"Stop. That's enough. You're a good mother. I know that whatever you did, you did out of love for Cody. Your past is over. I love you, in spite of and including what you've done. Let me help build a future for both of you. I can't promise that I'll be the greatest, but I'll be the best husband and father that I can be."

Lowering her head, she pressed her forehead against his chest, then raised her head to look at him, a smile brightening her eyes again. "I do love you, and your best is more than I deserve."

"Not even close." Capturing her lips with his, Lucas gave the promise of his love.

"Mom?"

Together, Rachel and Lucas turned to see Cody outside the diner. Chocolate smeared beside his mouth and whipped cream tipped his nose. His grin replaced the missing cherry. "Are we going home?"

Lucas chuckled at the sight and the joy his answer brought him. "Yes, we're going home."

Cody let out a wild, "Yippee," and raced around the parking lot.

Laughing, Lucas pulled Rachel close again. "Promise me two things," he said while he watched Cody.

"Anything," Rachel answered, her own laughter pure.

"That we give that boy a little brother or sister."

Rachel's warm smile couldn't match the heat in her answer. "I'd like that. And the other?"

She'd been trouble, all right, but he would go through fire to keep her brand of trouble by his side. "Promise me you won't run again. Ever."

"No, not ever," she said softly, "except into your arms."

* * * * *

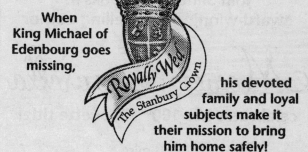

100th BOOK

Join Silhouette Books as award-winning, bestselling author

Marie Ferrarella

celebrates her 100th Silhouette title!

Don't miss
ROUGH AROUND THE EDGES
Silhouette Romance #1505
March 2001

To remain in the United States, Shawn O'Rourke needed a wife. Kitt Dawson needed a home for herself and the baby daughter Shawn had helped her deliver. A marriage of convenience seemed the perfect solution—until they discovered that the real thing was *much* more appealing than playacting....

Available at your favorite retail outlet.

Silhouette®

Where love comes alive™

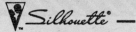

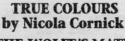
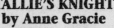